Forbidden

Forgiveness

by

Flenardo

Published and Edited by
    Creolistic Ink Publishing
    Destrehan, LA 70047

ISBN:
    9780578456553

<u>DEDICATION</u>

In memory of the warriors surviving and
fighting the cure for Cancer.

To all my readers & supporters patiently
waiting for this release. It's time to have
another gushy escapade. Flip the pages and
we shall squirt lyrical orgasms together.

Prelude

Malakai opens his eyes in darkness with a throbbing headache. His breathing shortens and focuses on how the goodness of pussy have caused his downfall.

He senses the nakedness as he feels a cool breeze under his balls.

He attempts to swing his body back and forward. He cannot move his hands nor feet. Someone has hogtied and suspended him in the air.

He recalls the excitement from this position in his *Poetic Whore* days. He used to fuck with a dominatrix who loved dangerous and kinky shit.

His flashback was short lived when the door creeps open followed by two male voices. The first voice speaks to the second one, "Pull the bag off that nigga and let's see if he's breathing."

The second voice lowers Malakai to waist level, unties and slides the bag off his face. He inhales the fresh air but remains silent with eyes closed. He mentally recites carnal sin number one. "Never let your enemy exploit your weakness."

The first assailant picks up a bucket of water and splashes Malakai's face and shouts, "Wake your bitch ass up!"

Malakai shakes his head, opens his eyes and instructs, "Tell Corbin I'm through playing these kiddie games."

They laugh as the first assailant drops the bucket and slaps his face. "You can't order anyone around. What the fuck we look like, one of your hoes? Oh, I forgot you don't have them."

The other assailant punches Malakai in the face. "That's for fucking my wife," he exclaims.

Malakai laughs and responds, "Your punches are weak as hell, no wonder she gave up the ass."

He balls his fist and ready to swing again before the first assailant stops him. "Don't waste your time on this idiot, we have big plans for him. It's time to put his mangy ass to sleep…Permanently."

The second assailant places the bag over Malakai's head and walks out.

He knows he can't stay in this position for long and need to escape. He overhears loud clacking coming from the hallway. The smell of a Cuban cigar lingers with the irritating and screeching sounds of fingernails scratching a chalkboard then it halts.

The second assailant snatches the bag so Malakai can see who's responsible.

Sitting in the chair is a woman in a ski mask wearing a dark skirt, white blouse and a pair of black stretch *Gianvito* ankle bootie.

She puffs and blows the smoke in his face. He coughs a few times and turns his head to avoid the smell.

She sinks her nails deep into his chin while blood slides down her finger. She places the tip in her mouth and sucks his blood greedily.

Her familiar *Dolce & Gabbana* scent drifts under his nose. He lifts his head and smiles, "I see you are wearing my favorite perfume."

She smiles with anticipation as he discovers she is here to end his life.

She pulls off the mask and asks, "Did you miss me?"

His refusal to answer aggravates her more. She sinks her nails deeper, "Keep being silent and I will cut out your tongue."

He speaks in a sluggish tone, "Death is better than being betrayed by the woman you love; kill me.

Chapter 1

1 Year Ago

Malakai drops his phone once the baby head pierces through Asperilla vagina.

"Oh Shit! Come on baby, a few more pushes. Our baby girl is almost here," he coaches.

"This is like an *Alien* movie. Asperilla you should see this monster busting through your pussy," he shouts.

"Mal...akai, Imma kill you," she babbles while breathing.

"Hell, you said the same shit during anal sex last week," he reminds her.

"Wait a minute, I have the perfect theme song," he yells and retrieves his phone from the floor.

"Ahhh! Get him the fuck out!" Asperilla screams.

Malakai plays *Push It* by *Salt-N-Pepa* and sings the chorus in the delivery room.

Oooh, baby, baby
Baby, baby
Oooh, baby, baby
Baby, baby
Get up on this!
Ah, push it
Ah, push it
Ah, push it (ow, get up on this)
Ah, push it (get up on this)

The doctor waves his hand to interrupt Malakai talent show. "Sir, can you please tone it down so she can focus?"

Malakai raises his hand to his temple and gives a military salute. "Yes sir!"

The delivery room returns to a state of normality and Malakai cheers Asperilla during her final stage.

"We are almost there, just one last push," the doctor confirms.

The doctor unravels the umbilical cord around the baby's neck allowing her head to rotate. Asperilla senses the freedom of relief as the baby slides out her womb.

There wasn't a sound for a few seconds as everyone anticipates Graciana first cry. Her little scream brought tears and smiles to their faces.

The doctor cleans her airways and passes Malakai the scissors. He wraps the baby and passes her to Asperilla. "Aww, you are so beautiful," she proclaims while crying and kissing her forehead. "Mami will love you forever."

"Baby, I'm going to step outside and let everyone know you and the baby are fine."

"Okay, we love you." Asperilla responds.

Malakai exits and finds the team anxious for the news. He shouts and jumps, "It's a girl!" He grabs an unknown female and kisses her, "I'm a fucking dad!"

"When can we go back there?" Isabella asks with her arm folded across her chest.

"I'm sure you all can visit shortly."

His phone vibrates during their conversation. "Excuse me, this is important. I'll be right back."

He taps his passcode and texts a few friends.

He smiles and throws his hand in the air. "Thank you, God, for allowing me to experience this moment."

He switches screens and dials an old friend. "Good afternoon, I'm ready to cash in my favor," he reminds.

"This is a dangerous one Malakai. There's a chance you won't make it out alive if things go wrong," she says.

"Yeah, the thought has crossed my mind numerous times," he reiterates.

"We are traveling outside the country in a few months, but I will touch basis with you weekly."

"By the way, how's Asperilla?"

"So much talk about business, I almost forgot to mention we are adding a baby girl to our family."

"Hey, are you there," he asks.

"Yeah, I'm here."

"Okay, for a minute I thought you hung up."

"No, I was thinking about your good news. Please give Asperilla my love."

"I will handle everything on my end. Enjoy your vacation."

Malakai ends the call and walks back to Asperilla's room. "Daddy is back, where's the after-birth party?" He jokes.

Asperilla face cringes. "Eww, you are so damn nasty."

Malakai kisses her hand. "Today we are complete."

Chapter 2

Ms. Drummond kicks the desk and throws her pen to the floor. "Mr. Lancaster! Have you heard anything I said pertaining to Malakai?"

He jerks from his trance, adjusts his tie and shifts his attention to the papers. "Ms. Drummond, please excuse my rudeness. Can we conduct this meeting another day?"

Ms. Drummond arches her eyebrows and gives him the side eye. "Sure, Mr. Lancaster."

She uncrosses her legs, lifts her briefcase and twists her hips toward the door.

Her sexy walk and long legs attracted the bulge in his pants. He rushes from his seat and blows his minted breath on her neck.

"Spread your legs," he commands.

She releases everything she was holding and slide steps to provide full access.

He squats, lifts her skirt, massages and sucks on her vanilla thighs. He cradles and kisses each ass cheek. "Aww, I love when you come to work panty less," he whispers.

"Yes, my juices are dripping on the wooden floor," she moans submissively.

He humps her from behind, allowing her to feel the thickness in his pants.

He gently moves her hair over her right ear. "Susan, forgive me for being out of rhythm today," he speaks apologetically. "My routine is off from skipping lunch. Will you be the cure for my hunger? My tongue is ready to dance on your clitoris."

He drops to his knees, pokes his nose between her thighs and inhales.

He lubricates two fingers with saliva and gently glide them in her moist opening.

She spreads her legs wider and clamps her muscle over his thick fingers. "Go deeper," she moans.

He adores making her beg while he makes love.

"Susan."

"Yes, Corbin."

He stretches his arm with an open palm and slaps her right ass cheek.

"Do it again," she whines.

The intense of watching her squeal increases the blood in his vein and the fire in his eyes. He yanks her hair with his fist. "What's my name?"

"Mr. Lancaster! Mr. Lancaster!" she yells from the depth of her lungs.

He slaps her ass again. "You haven't earned that right yet," he scolds.

"Yes sir! Please forgive me for my defiance and let me make it up," she vows.

She descends to her knees, unfastens his pants and slides the zipper down.

Corbin wiggles his hips while she tugs on his pants. He drops his pants and underwear to his ankles.

She smiles devilishly at his erected shaft and worships his mushroom tip.

Corbin grabs her head. "Put it in your mouth."

Susan expands her jaws and his dick slithers to the back of her throat. She glides her mouth in reverse and slurps precum and drool simultaneously.

He wraps his fist around her hair and pumps his dick into her mouth. His pelvic bounces against her forehead as she gags but knows not to upset him.

He fucks her mouth and she used her fingers to play musical notes in her slit.

"Baby your mouth is glorious."

He scoops her in his arms and carries her to the desk.

She reaches between his thighs and caresses his dick. "I want it all."

"Are you sure?"

"Yes, my body is yours for the taking."

He inserts the tip in her pussy until nothing is left but his balls.

Corbin indulges in her wetness while pressing her head against the desk. He repositions himself and plows through her.

"Oh, Mr. Lancaster it feels so good," she whimpers.

He cranks his inner strength, sinks his teeth into her right shoulder blades and thrusts deeper. Sweat drips from his forehead and lands on her spine.

"Cum with me Ms. Drummond," he demands.

She clinches his dick for a sensational and pulsating rush. She rocks backwards and bangs her ass against his thighs.

He grabs her waist and thrusts faster. Her legs tremble and she yells, "I'm cum…ming."

She bites her bottom lip as her orgasm ricochets through her walls. Her facial expression causes him to roar like a ferocious lion. He increases the impact and her pussy defies him by talking back when he smacks against it.

He stands on his tiptoes and rams her one last time. His nut skeets like a geyser. He fills her with love seeds, yanks it out and shoots the rest on her butt cheeks. He admires his cum dripping art like *Pablo Picasso*.

He lifts her in his arm and stares into her eyes. "Care to join me for a shower?"

She nods her head in agreement because her mouth couldn't say a word.

Chapter 3

"This place is gorgeous; exactly how I pictured my life after robbing you," Asperilla jokes.

She lifts Graciana near her breast and glances at Malakai. "If it wasn't for love, I would have annihilated your ass."

He chuckles and blows her a kiss. "Thanks for sparing a whore a doghouse in your queendom."

"The penthouse is perfect, and the *Indian Ocean* is outside our bedroom window. We have a personal gym and chef."

"I'm glad you love *Kenya* and it a relaxing getaway from Tampa. No drama, no police, no- "

"And no groupies trying to kill us," Asperilla interrupts. "Necole was crazy in love with you and you better not attend an open mic while we are here."

"Graciana inherited your breast sucking skills."

"Wow, with her greedy ass."

"Speaking of being greedy, why haven't we fucked? Do you find me less attractive?"

He kisses her lips, "No, you are as beautiful as ever."

He chooses his words carefully and respects her sentimental feelings. He pulls down his shorts and presents his dick. "You always turn me on baby."

He slaps his dick and chants, "Arise o' great beast. You are summoned tonight to battle. Her land has not been invaded and you have been chosen to devour her milk and honey. Send Zeus' mouthpiece to make her orgasm strike like lighting and her toes crack like thunder. Give my dick the hardest armor on the planet as I prepare for war."

He slaps his dick again and grow inches as she watches his performance.

Asperilla laughs and says, "You are stupid but do it again."

He pounds his chest and rubs his shaft. "Rise, I tell you."

He tilts his head in the air and speaks in a narrative voice like *James Earl Jones*. "You have awakened me from my abyss and tonight I shall dine on your blood."

She pats Graciana's back and cuts her eye towards Malakai. "Good because I'm on my period and I have a blood bank for you to suck with your *Blade* wannabe ass," she jokes.

"Damn you can fuck up a mood with your nasty ass," he insists.

He kicks a chair and utters with a pout, "You wasted my Oscar-nominated performance and you're on your cycle."

She throws a pillow to his head. "Fool, I was only joking. You think I'm going to turn down a nut after three months. You better summon Buddha, Jesus, Prophet Muhammad and the Devil. I plan on fucking the life from you."

He runs over, kisses her lips and grips her ass.

"Mmm, I am riding your face when Grace goes to sleep."

"You two are the most important people in my world," he notes.

"More than poetry?"

"Fuck poetry!"

"I'll fantasize while you are sleeping."

"You're an asshole, I knew you couldn't give her up."

"For the record, I wasn't always a *Poetic Whore*. There was a time I wanted to be in the NBA."

She repositions comfortably to hear this long tale about shoulda, coulda and woulda.

Malakai spots a piece of paper a few feet for him. "Watch this since you doubt me."

He crumbles the paper, arches his arm and releases. The paper floats in slow motion, Malakai celebrates prematurely, and the paper misses the trash can by 2 feet.

Asperilla explodes with laughter, "You shoot worse than Lonzo Ball."

He gets another sheet and balls it up. "Here you try it, with your smart mouth," he challenges.

"Hold her and watch a real ballplayer. Step back and you might learn something today," she taunts.

"Let's see what you got and how about we make a small wager."

She flips her hair and bends down to touch her toes.

"What the fuck you are doing? It doesn't take all that to shoot a basket."

She jiggles her ass before turning around, "If I win, I'm going to lick your ass and use a vibrator while sucking your dick."

She flings the paper from her fingertips and glides it in the air.

Malakai prays she misses the shot until it bounces off the side of the can and drops in.

She does her *Steph Curry* impersonation; lifting her legs in the air and walking like a British guard.

She gyrates her hips in circles, squatting and making her ass wiggle before bolting inside the penthouse.

"Damn it," Malakai mumbles in defeat.

He brushes off Asperilla victory and kisses Graciana. She yawns and her sparkling eyes glaze upon his.

"Good Afternoon Graciana, I'm sure your Mami's crazy victory dance woke you up."

He gives her a tour of the landscape and beautiful ocean. "I can't wait to bring you back to the Motherland when you are older."

"Asperilla, where are you?"

"Here I come baby."

Asperilla runs onto the yard in a two-piece bikini set with pom- poms.

"Give me an a… s… s… hole. Eating your ass until you beg for mercy."

She jumps and lands in a split.

"Asperilla, you better get off the ground before a bug crawl in your chocho."

She springs to her feet. "You haven't used my favorite word in years. When she goes to sleep, we are fucking," she informs by slapping her crotch.

"How about we make love under the stars?"

"Ahem, keep the romantic shit. I want cum in all my holes."

Malakai moves closer and plucks her lips anticipating a juicy kiss. He bypasses her lips and whispers in her ear, "She is hungry and so am I."

"I have plenty of pussy to force down your throat."

Malakai and Asperilla swap Graciana and he fetch the chef to create a special dish.

Asperilla hugs her, "Your life will be better than mine. You will never have to struggle, watch your mother sell pussy or involved in anything illegal. I will protect and kill for you."

A single tear drops from her eyelid and lands on Graciana face. "I'm sorry baby. Mommy's emotions are getting the best of her."

She swipes the running tear with her index finger and places it on her tongue. "Umm, so this is what love tastes like. "Let's find your Papi and enjoy this beautiful afternoon."

Chapter 4

Malakai rocks Graciana in his chair listening to *Sade* and admiring her smile. "Little lady, it's time for you to go to sleep."

She smiles again and flashes her dimples like her Mother.

"I know you are waiting for me to sing but I spit poetry. You better recognize who you are dealing with," he warns.

She erupts in a loud scream alerting she's not in the mood for his shit.

"Ok, ok; hush little baby don't you cry," he sings.

Malakai stands from the chair, walks to the radio and turn the volume down a little.

He bounces her with every step until her cries are calm. "Ok, little lady, you win again."

Malakai inhales air from the pit of his stomach and sings her favorite note.

> *"No need to ask, he's a smooth operator*
> *Smooth operator, smooth operator*
> *Coast to coast, LA to Chicago, western male*
> *Across the north and south, to Key Largo, love for* sale
> *Smooth operator, smooth operator*
> *Smooth operator, smooth operator"*

He paces from the den to the kitchen, repeating the same verse before her eyelids drift to la la land. He treads lightly and places her in the *Intellicot*.

He shakes his head in disbelief from the crib's expensive price tag. With a little convincing from Asperilla, he fell in love with it.

It has a mattress-raising system to reduce strain on her back, air circulation to keep her cool, a soft blue nightlight and a video monitoring system so he can watch her from another room. He wonders what a baby dreams while watching her lie in perfect harmony.

He spins around and Asperilla stands in a guipure lace bra and panty set. The lace embroidered trim around her breasts and neckline gives a teasing but dramatic effect. The matching high-waisted panty features a provocative tie-up front and sheer seductive mesh wraps around the back.

She bats her eyelashes, claps her heels and twirls like a little school girl. She licks her lips. "Do you like what you see?" She asks inquisitively.

"I don't like; I love your glistening skin, your hair down your back, sexy earrings and your freshly shaved pussy."

She grabs him by the shirt, "Shut up and kiss me."

Malakai lifts her and she coils her legs around his waist.

He parts his tongue through her lips and interweaves sticky saliva with no breaks. He flushes his tongue down her throat, gripping his nails in her ass cheeks and humping against her crotch.

She feels his erection on her navel. She breaks the kiss. "Fuck me Papi."

He carries her to the bedroom, undress, and reveals his rippled abs and smooth dark chocolate skin.

She licks her fingers before rubbing them over her clit. "Mmm, come and eat," she invites by waving her drenched fingers.

He rushes and plants his face between her thighs. "Give me this sweet pussy,"

His teeth clamp on her harden clit as he swiftly slides one finger into her pussy and the other one in her asshole.

"Yes, baby! All my doors are ready for you."

She thrust wildly in the air, wrapping her hands around his head and violently fucks his face.

"Eat this pussy you nasty Punta!"

Malakai grunts louder, breaks free and slurps her perineum.

"Oh, shit baby, do it again," she screams.

He bites her inner thigh, slides down and blows in her asshole.

She grabs his head and moans, "I wanna ride your face."

He sucks her clit again before flipping on his back.

She squats and grinds over his nose and mouth. "Bitch, I'm going to cum in your eyes. I need this nut, I'm going to teach you to not make me wait another three months."

She grabs his head, leans back and bounces harder. "I'm gonna suffocate your ass," she threatens.

He pulls back, spits on her clit and eats faster. He slaps her ass and she increase her speed.

"You like tasting this gushy shit?"

"Grrrr," he growls.

Her pussy smacks his lips and his tongue go deeper to meet her bounce.

She wiggles her waist. "Don't stop! Oh shit, I'm cumming. Baby I'm… I'm… I'm."

She spreads her pussy wider and releases the hardest orgasm ever. Flooding his face until juices run behind his ears.

He squeezes her ass cheeks, preventing her from escaping as he sucks harder and faster. She tries to break free, but he holds tighter.

She slaps his face repeatedly before he let her go.

"Dammit Malakai, you know my pussy sensitive after I cum, you play too much. Ole bitch ass!"

"You weren't worrying about sensitivity when you were trying to drown me."

She spins, lands on her knees and twerk her ass in the air. "Beat it!"

He strokes his dick before ramming into her.

She throws her ass back to meet his thrusts.

"Oh, you think you hanging with this dick."

He grabs her by the throat, pulls her closer and fuck her stronger. He slides his index finger into her wet pussy, pulls it out and allow her to taste her juices.

Pushing her into the bed and causing her knees to collapse, he climbs on top and plunges. "You want it? Say you want this dick!"

"Give it to me,' she yells.

The sex intensifies as he rapidly pumps faster.

"Baby, I'm about to cum. Oh Shit, this the best pussy ever. Clench my dick bitch. Clench my fucking dick," he orders.

She squeezes her muscles tightly with determination to milk the monster. The pressure builds, his body shakes and he pulls her hair for leverage.

"Here I cum.".

The warmness shoots like mini rockets and explodes inside her. He pulls out, plants his face between her thighs and sucks his left over from her snack box. He savors some in his mouth, and swap kisses unifying their love. He breaks the kiss, turns over and Asperilla rests her head on his chest.

She pinches his nipples while he pulls the strings in her hair.

"I love you, baby."

"Love you too boo."

She slides her legs between his and says, "I'll wait until my pussy stop pulsating before round two."

He glances at the videocam on the nightstand to make sure they haven't awakened Graciana.

"Take your time baby, she's still asleep."

"Good, because I plan on draining your ass before sunrise."

They share a laugh and another kiss before the next round.

Chapter 5

"Good Evening, everything we discuss is strictly confidential and must not leave this room," Corbin briefs. "Do I make myself clear?"

The panel replies, "Yes Mr. Lancaster."

He tugs the knot on his tie, takes a seat and ask for the daily report.

Ms. Drummond springs from her seat and passes out the secret files to everyone at the roundtable. She grabs the remote and turns on the smart TV displaying Malakai's picture.

"If you all will kindly turn to page one and follow along." She scans the room to assure everyone was in sync before changing the screen.

"As you all can see, Malakai appears as a legitimate club owner and artist. Everything is a front for his secret escort operations."

She flips to the next image displaying Asperilla. The men in the room gloated over her long pretty hair and hypnotizing eyes.

One of the lawyers' coughs while drinking his water, interrupting the brief.

Ms. Drummond places her hands on her hips. "Will someone please slap him on the back."

The detective sitting next to him slaps the lawyer and his forehead hits the table.

The detective smirks and asks, "Are you alright?"

The lawyer responds, "Hell no and don't touch me again."

"Fine! I'll let you die next time."

"Fuck you."

Corbin jumps from his seat and snaps, "If you two interrupt my meeting again, I will toss you out my office windows and watch your body plummet fourteen floors. Now sit your ass down and don't say shit until I give you permission to speak."

"Yes Sir."

Corbin returns to his seat and spirals his fingers in the air as a gesture for Ms. Drummond to proceed with the briefing.

"Now that we are back in order. As you can see Asperilla has a unique effect on men. Charming and killing within a blink of an eye. Malakai and Asperilla are public enemy number one and they belong on death row for all the horrendous crimes committed. You all are here because we are seeking subject matter experts in corruption, planting evidence and extortion," she admits.

Ms. Drummond mutes the TV and faces the room. "Are there any questions?"

The detective asks, "Are we getting paid for this because it wasn't mentioned in the briefing?"

Corbin taps his pencil on his desk before breaking it in half. He scoots his chair back and addresses the room. "Everyone wants to get paid but let's not forget the times I have saved everyone ass in here once or twice. All I'm asking is for your cooperation and the reward will be great once I become Governor for taking down the city infamous whoremonger."

Corbin smiles knowing power and greed arouse their hormones every time.

"My father always said if a man can't accept your business agreement with a simple handshake than he is better off dead."

"We are going to setup Malakai with an underage escort. Once he falls for the bait, we will seize his assets, and arrest him for statutory rape."

The rooms erupt in chatters and congratulations after hearing Corbin's bulletproof plan.

The office door opens to an exquisite African American woman dressed in a cream long sleeve business bodysuit.

She removes her sunglasses and places the tip in her mouth. Her demeanor commands attention from every head in the room and she knows it.

"Who the hell you think you are for disrupting my meeting?" Corbin asks.

She swivels her foot on the ball of her heel. "My name isn't your concern and I hate to swallow your pre-ejaculation party."

Corbin runs his fingers through his hair. "All the money I spend on security and they don't check badges for shit. Ms. Drummond make sure they are replaced before morning."

"Yes Mr. Lancaster."

Corbin walks to the office door. "Everyone, please leave so I can speak to this woman alone."

They exit swiftly and he closes the door after the last person.

He turns around and the mysterious woman has her finger on the trigger of a *Crimson Trace LG-431 Laserguard* with the red laser pointing at his chest.

The mysterious woman strolls around Corbin in circles. "Are you afraid to die Corbin?"

"Not at all, it will bring me closer to the woman I love," he responds and blows her a kiss.

She squeezes the trigger slowly. "Nighty Night muthafucker," she says.

Corbin places one hand in his pocket and stands upright.

The gun goes click and he never flinches.

She leans over and kisses his forehead.

"Corbin Lancaster, either you are brave or crazy as hell, but we need each other's service."

She scribbles her hotel address on the notepad, rips it, and shove the content inside his pants.

She gathers her things, strolls down the hall, and disappears behind the elevator door.

Chapter 6

Corbin weaves through traffic until he approaches the *Marriott Waterside Hotel & Marina*. He coasts to the valet, grabs his *Beretta U2*, and the ticket number from the attendant.

He walks through the hotel lobby and the mysterious woman from his office is sitting at the bar sipping on a martini.

She sits her glass on the stand and pats her hand on the seat next to her. "Have a seat."

"Oh, now you are being ladylike after disrupting my meeting."

She sips her drink, licks her lips and stares between his legs. "If you play your cards right, I'll make it up to you."

"Mr. Lancaster, would you like something to drink."

"No thank you. I rather know what I can do for you."

She runs her tongue around the glass, guzzles the drink and erupts with a loud burp.

"Eww! You dress like a lady, but you are nothing more than a thot."

He stands, peels some cash and tips the bartender. "Enjoy your evening."

She adjusts her dress. "Nope, never a thot Mr. Lancaster. I'm gutty as they come, and you need me."

"Need you, bitch is you serious? Do you know who you are dealing with? I could have you behind prison walls within seconds."

"Yep, you could, but you will never get Malaki without me."

"What the fuck do you know about Malakai?"

"Everything; follow me and we can speak in private."

She leads him around the corner and ride the elevators to the rooftop. She spins in a circle and inhales the night air. "Dance with me," she says reaching for Corbin's hand.

He slaps it away. "I don't have time for games."

She walks toward the balcony and swings her legs over the ledge.

"I should push her ass off the ledge and clean it up as a suicide but her knowledge on Malakai might be helpful," he thinks.

He joins her on the ledge and breaks the ice. "Who are you and how do you know I wouldn't kill you?"

"Mr. Lancaster, life is filled with consequences and pussy rules the world."

"Call me Corbin."

"Hi Corbin, my name is Savior. I'm here to reclaim my throne and heal your pain."

Corbin drops his head to keep from laughing at his new acquaintance.

She chuckles along with him and slaps his legs. "I'm just fucking with you Corbin," she jokes.

"On a serious note, my name is Ayanna Robinson. I am the most sought out distinguished Assistant District Attorney in Atlanta. I was paid to infiltrate your team and report my findings to my boss. You were so occupied with Malakai you forgot you posted an ad for additional support. Your organization needs someone with sophistication and street sense. I'm the perfect candidate," she boasts.

"I have Ms. Drummond already," he mentions.

"Who? The white chick? Fuck her! She can't hold a candle to me, and you know it," she snickers in his face after her statement.

"Who is your boss?"

"Malakai."

Corbin loses his balance but regains his composure and exhale a deep breath.

"Breath baby, it's alright," she assures.

"Can we sit in a normal place to finish this discussion?"

"Sure, but wait a minute. Have you ever wanted to see how far spit will travel from high altitude?"

She hocks a wad in her mouth and drops it unto the crowd below.

She snaps her finger and raps. *Don't pull the thang out, unless you plan to bang. Bombs over Baghdad!*

"Ms. Ayanna, you are unique and gritty. I can respect your professional hoodness."

He extends his hand, pulls her from the ledge and escorts her to the seating area. "Now back to Malakai and his plan."

"Where was I?" She asks.

"You were discussing how you were going to infiltrate my team," he mentions.

"I'm not after your team anymore. Let's chat about what we can do for each other."

She kisses him on the cheek, "For the record Corbin, you are a sexy ass white man. I usually don't do white meat, but you can get it."

He blushes and realizes she may be alright after all.

'You are sexy yourself and I haven't encountered a black woman since Nik's death. Never mind," he pauses and drops his head.

"Go ahead and say it Corbin, you mean Nikki."

"How do you know her name?"

She raises her index finger. "Hold your thoughts for a second. If we are going to discuss this, we need more drinks."

She returns her attention. "You need balls of steel to go against Malakai."

"You don't think I can conquer him without you?"

"No, he will smell you a mile away and destroy your team one by one. Hell, your dick saw me coming before your brain. He operates through pussy."

"What do rich boys drink? Never mind, I'll order for you."

"Ok."

Corbin checks his watch. "I'm not getting anywhere with this woman."

She returns with the drinks. "Here you go; this is perfect. Let's sip and chat. I was going to infiltrate your business and send Malakai in to slaughter your ass," she confesses.

"What the fuck can you do for me then?"

She sips her drink and bites on the cherry. "Umm, this is good." She pauses for a moment and blurts, "I'll double cross him for you."

"You are super confident Ms. Robinson."

"I'm confident because I know his operation from head to toe."

"I want to oversee your operation and lead the assault. In the end, you will have his head and I'll have my revenge."

"What's your beef with him?"

"It's personal but when you are governor, you must promote me as the head district attorney."

He rubs his hand over her thighs. "I'll think about it overnight and contact you tomorrow."

She spreads her legs wide. "You sure you don't want to stay for the after-party."

He rinses his throat with the drink. "Nah I'm good baby maybe another time."

He walks toward the exit, pauses and asks another question. "How did you get on your level?"

"I am the original bottom bitch. The title carries weight in the street game. Call me tomorrow with your proposal."

He doesn't deal with orders easily, but they do share a common enemy. He presses the button on the elevator, returns to the lobby and retrieves his car.

He places the gun in the console and ponders her proposal as he drives home.

Chapter 7

Corbin didn't sleep well last night and shows up at the board meeting in his gym clothes.

He covers his mouth with his palm to block his yawn. "Excuse me for my tardiness, how's everyone doing today?"

The board witnesses Corbin's transformation from tailor suits to ankle socks, tank, and tennis shoes.

"Ms. Drummond, please continue with yesterday's briefing."

"Right away, Mr. Lancaster."

"Please turn to page five in your book and let's discuss the statutory rape charge."

"Ms. Drummond, do you think this will work?" Corbin asks.

"I believe so."

He snaps his pencil in half. "I need you to do more. Make me a believer, make us a believer. Will this plan bring Malakai to his knees?"

"Mr. Lancaster, I thought we agreed to work this concept."

"Have a seat, Ms. Drummond."

She slides in her seat, drops her head and pretends to work from her binder.

Corbin scratches his neck and springs from his seat. "I know we worked hard on this plan, but it sucks. I have decided to bring in reinforcements."

The room mumbles wondering who Corbin is appointing to take the lead.

"Excuse me but I'm speaking," he interrupts.

"The board will remain the same and Ms. Drummond?

"Yes, Mr. Lancaster," she responds without lifting her head from the desk.

"Make sure your new team chief is up to speed."

Corbin presses the button on the intercom, "Please escort Ms. Robinson to the meeting."

'Please accept my apology if I offended anyone but we have a chance to take down this monster once and for all. I'm not sure how long this window will stay open, so this drastic change is necessary," he explains.

Security opens the door and Ayanna comes in singing.
"I was born to flex (Yes)
Diamonds on my neck
I like boardin' jets, I like mornin' sex (Woo!)
But nothing in this world that I like more than checks (Money)
All I really wanna see is the (Money)
I don't really need the D, I need the (Money)
All a bad bitch need is the (Money)."

"Since I have made my grand entrance, allow me to reintroduce myself. I am ADA Ayanna Robinson. I have a Bachelor of Arts in Administration of Justice, Master's in Criminal Justice, and a PhD in Criminology and all from *Howard University*. I relocated as a legal apprentice in Atlanta under DA Lopez. I'm sure you heard about his 98% successful prosecution rate. Well the 90% belongs to me and I was quickly escalated to the top. I'm here because I want a piece of Tampa and you all are going to make sure I achieve the American dream."

Corbin stands and claps his hands. "I told you all she is suitable for the job," he congratulates.

Ayanna walks to the board and post pictures.

Ms. Drummond slides Ms. Robinson the remote. "You are free to use the Smart TV because posting pictures are ancient," she says.

Ayanna rejects her offer and continues to post pictures.

"The future always refers to the past for knowledge and you will be history without me," Ayanna mentions. "Last night I took the liberty to do minor research and it appears you all are criminals. Great, we all have something in common. We are here for one purpose and one purpose only to eradicate Malakai and Asperilla Valdez. You all are correct, the club is being used for money laundering, but you will never be able to prove it. Let's focus on tearing the head off the snake. Malakai has never had a weakness until now. The birth of his little girl has shaken his empire. I need everyone to write their phone numbers and addresses," she mentions and a sheet of paper across the table. "In the meantime, find a hobby until I call you."

A few board members stand and object her wishes. "We don't trust you and refuse to relinquish our authority."

The team wonder if Corbin will stop this fiasco. He doesn't budge from his seat and appears fascinated by her presentation.

Ayanna stands firmly in her decisions. "Maybe we started the wrong way this morning. Please forgive me for coming in here rapping *Cardi B*. I knew you were some uptight bitches and I wanted to liven up this boring meeting. You don't hate my leadership. You hate I'm a black woman in charge. Today is your lucky day, you are free to go. I'll get the information on my own. If you cross me, it will be bloodshed and consequences."

"Fuck this shit I'm out! If you all were smart you would leave too before she leads you to an early grave."

Everyone leaves the room except Ayanna, Corbin, & Ms. Drummond.

Ayanna and Ms. Drummond eyes connect and neither speaks a word.

"We are the three musketeers; the weak links have left the room," he proclaims.

Ms. Drummond flashes a fake smile knowing she can't stand Ayanna but refuses for another bitch to steal her work.

They return to the backboard and strategize the next move. Ayanna pins a picture of Asperilla holding Graciana on the board. "You can have Malakai and Asperilla, but the baby belongs to me."

Ms. Drummond arches her eyebrows and wonders why she is obsessed with the baby. They work endless hours combining resources to eliminate Malakai.

Corbin visualizes fucking Ayanna as she works on the case. He's determined to taste her pussy before the end of the week.

"Excuse me but today has been a long one. May I get you all something to drink?" Corbin suggests.

For the first time, they are on the same page.

"Sure!" They shout.

He retrieves a bottle of *Dom Perignon* and three glasses. He pours and passes them around.

"Death to Malakai," He salutes.

They toast and continue working throughout the evening.

Chapter 8

Ayanna stands and takes a deep stretch. "Ahh, I think my job is done tonight."

She slings her purse over her shoulder and scrolls to the door.

Corbin races to congratulate her. "Thanks for your help and I'll contact you later this week."

Ayanna gives Corbin a gigantic hug, massage his shoulders and winks toward Ms. Drummond. She knows how to antagonize a person by stealing her position and Corbin's attention in one evening.

Ayanna exits the workplace with a smile. *"Did I feel Corbin's dick against my thigh?"* She pushes her horny desires away and rides the elevator to the parking deck.

The door opens, and she rambles through her purse to her car. She pulls out the keys and presses the unlock button.

Working for Malakai all these years have strengthened her survival senses. A white male approaches her driver side door. She remains calm and plays a damsel in distress.

She lifts the handle and opens the door. A white hand appears over her shoulders and slams it back. "Where the hell you think you are going?" He asks.

His stinky cologne flares through her nostril.

She remains silent so he can talk.

"You think you are big shit because Mr. Lancaster promoted you above us. You are nothing but a ghetto ass nigger with a college degree."

She recognizes the familiar voice from the man protesting her position in the board meeting.

She squeezes the remote key in her hand tighter and anxious to punch him in the throat.

"I guess I'll be ladylike," she thinks.

"Sir, it has been a long night and if you don't mind, could you please step away from my car?"

"If I don't, what the fuck are you going to do?"

"Fuck me, another fake gangster in a business suit," she mumbles.

She pleads a second time hoping he will leave her alone.

"I will forgive you for calling me out my name. Maybe your mother never taught a peasant how to respect royalty. I will ask you nicely and this is my final warning."

She inches closer to his face. "Step the fuck away from my door."

"And what if- "

Ayanna jabs the key in his neck and yanks it out.

Her swift attack causes him to stumble and trample to the concrete. He rolls back and forth, applying his palm against his neck for pressure.

"Help! Someone help me," he screams.

She giggles as she creeps toward him. "No one can hear you down here. It's just you and me. I did ask you to leave me alone. I should leave you here to bleed but I'm going to make an example out of your punk ass," she reminds him and stomps his chest.

She dials Corbin's number and places him on speakerphone. "Thanks for letting me know you made it home."

She stares at the ground for a moment. "No, I never left the parking garage. I met a friend from the meeting," she responds.

"Who?"

"Mr. Talkative. It seems he wanted to discuss business outside normal hours."

"Ayanna, are you ok?"

"I'm fine but your associate isn't."

"What did you do?" Corbin inquiries. "Never mind, I'll be down there in a minute."

His adrenaline causes him to bypass the elevators and explode through the first stairwell exit. He opens the door to the parking deck dripping sweat and breathing heavily. He leans over, placing his hands on his thighs, and mentally count numbers to slow down his heart rate.

After regaining his poise, he stands upright and screams, "Ayanna! Where are you?"

"I'm over here. Come see the blood gushing from his neck."

He sprints through the parking deck searching for her voice.

"Mr. Lancaster, you passed right by us. We are over here on the ground."

He halts, turns around and shell-shocked from the scene. "What the fuck Ayanna?"

"I asked him nicely to leave me alone. "He's lucky he can smell because I was going to cut off his nose."

Corbin pats his pocket for his phone. "Shit! I left it upstairs. Ayanna show some concern, call 911."

She tosses her phone. "Catch, you call them, I'm going home."

"You have no damn heart and I'm going to stop being a gentleman around your ass."

"That's exactly what I want you to do. Remember you need balls of steel to fuck with Malakai," she reminds him and walks to her car.

She starts the ignition and rolls down the window. "Corbin show some compassion, hurry up; he needs medical attention," she mocks.

She stomps the gas pedal causing her tires to screech out the parking deck.

"Crazy bitch," he groans. "This all your fault Ron. You should have left her alone."

"Fuck her," he mutters between his teeth.

Corbin dials his office phone and before Ms. Drummond could answer he speaks quickly. "Susan, bring my medical box to the parking garage ASAP."

They disconnect the call and he stares at his old business associate. "Be a fucking man, you are lucky to be alive."

Corbin takes his shirt and applies pressure to Ron's neck. "Hold still, help is on the way."

Ms. Drummond arrives with the necessary items. "Here's everything you requested."

"Thank you."

"Ms. Drummond, please apply pressure while I sterilize the utensils."

"What are you going to do?" Ron asks.

"Stitch your wound. Now leave me the hell alone before I change my mind."

"Ms. Drummond, stop applying pressure." She removes the bloody shirt and Corbin douses Ron with alcohol.

"Aww shit!!" he screams.

Corbin chuckles and says, "Sorry man, I meant to grab the peroxide."

Corbin stitches Ron's wound and provides relief until the ambulance arrives.

Chapter 9

Ayanna alarm rings for the second time. She stretches her hand and tap the off button.

After the incident with Corbin's associates, she's not accepting negative energy in her world today.

She rises out of the bed, slide on her slippers and opens the patio door. She steps outside fully nude, febreezing the air with her scented juices. She saunters to the kitchen to brew green coffee.

She loves her condo on the beach, and it amazes her how she hid it from Asperilla and Malakai.

Her phone vibrates on the island countertop "Damn this nigga is like clockwork," she mutters.

"Good Morning."

"What's good Ayanna? How's the assignment?"

'Things are going well. Corbin is weak minded and easy to manipulate. You should have seen their faces when I interrupted their business meeting with my triumph entrance."

"It sounds like you are enjoying this thrill more than I expected. You should move on him before they start to suspect your motives."

"Damn Malakai why are you dead serious these days. I remember you used to have fun planning new kills."

"I don't want to kill Corbin; only cripple his obsession and finances against me. Plus, it's hard to be humorous when you are protecting your wife and child."

The weird vibe between them is interrupted by the kettle pot whistle.

"Malakai hold on for one second."

She mutes the phone and takes a deep breath. "I'm not bringing negative energy around me," she mumbles.

"How's Asperilla and the baby?'

"They are wonderful. We are adjusting to this new lifestyle. I don't sleep a lot these days."

"Welcome to parenthood."

"Yeah, being a father is a blessing and stressful."

"When are you all coming back to the states," she interrupts his precious moment.

"I'm not sure. Stop asking me all these questions and produce the records," he vents and exhales through the phone.

"Dammit, I fucked up. I need to contemplate quickly. Malakai, I apologize for rubbing you the wrong way. I asked because a few girls recognized me and wanted to know about your next performance," she explains.

"I haven't been in the performing mood lately but send them my love. Please enjoy your day. I'm not an asshole but have a lot on my mind. I'll be in touch next week."

She ends the call and sips her tea. "Shit! I better watch my tongue with his ass."

Malakai has never known Ayanna to question his judgments, maybe he's overthinking things. He doesn't own her, and she doesn't work for him anymore. He let it go and rotate the focus to his wife and child.

He rises from his seat only to be pushed down. *"What the fuck,"* he wonders. "Damn, how long have you been standing there?"

"Enough to hear you and Ayanna plotting against me!"

"Please calm down. No one is plotting anything."

She slaps his face. "Don't fucking play with me. How long have you two been fooling around? Oh, you're not going to answer me. Alright, I'll be right back."

She runs into the house and returns with her Glock 19.

"I bet you open your mouth now or my baby and I will be fatherless today," she blurts.

"Alright, put the gun away before you accidentally shoot me in the head."

He takes a deep sigh and goes in on the details. "Please listen; no one is cheating and you're the only woman I need."

He attempts to kiss her, but she slaps him for the second time.

"Save the love and romantic bullshit for later. What's going on with these secret phone calls? I hope you didn't think I would be too occupied with Graciana and wouldn't notice shit."

Malakai massages his cheeks. "I can't remember the last time you slap the shit out of me. You want the truth, okay. After Nikki's murder, I knew Corbin would seek revenge and I wanted to strike first. I apologize for keeping you in the dark about the secret phone calls. I sent Ayanna to gather his financial records and put him away forever without killing him."

"Why didn't you tell me all this shit before? You are always trying to be a superhero behind my back. Last time I checked, it was me saving your life," she reminds him with a punch to his chest.

"I should have left you chained in the basement with your groupie. Ayanna hasn't been down with us for a few years. What makes you think we can trust her now? She left the game and became a big shot attorney in Atlanta. I don't trust bitches who stop selling pussy to go legit and I'm about to stop trusting your bitch ass. If you really want to protect us, find the old Malakai because this one ain't shit. You are going to get us all killed. Fuck the secret ops, just walk up and put a bullet in his head. I'm exhausted from traveling. I want to sleep in my own home, go shopping, and live my exquisite life. Are you scared to go home?"

Malakai didn't respond. Instead, he stared at the sky and ignored her statement.

"Fuck you Malakai," she yells while throwing her hands in the air and walking away.

She returns with a pen and pad. "Here's your bitch. Tonight, you and poetry can sleep outside. The plane will be refueled in the morning and I'm leaving with or without your ass," she responds and walk away.

"All I want is to do things the correct way and keep my nose clean. Fuck you Asperilla! I'll stay out all damn night. It will be sunrise before I come back to this muthafucker."

His anger for her made him realize he forgot to kiss his daughter.

"Asperilla is right but I'm not telling her a damn thing."

He run to the nursery and finds Asperilla rocking Graciana to sleep.

"I love you," he whispers.

Asperilla didn't respond but rolls her eyes. Oh okay

He kisses them, "Since tonight is my last night, I'm going out."

She shrugs her shoulders and enunciates slowly in his face, "I don't give a fuck."

She flickers her hand and shews him away.

"I can't deal with this shit right now. I'm out."

He knows the sleeping whore ready to be woken. He used to fuck bitches as a stress release but now he must find positive things to keep him entertained."

He won't get in trouble tonight but will create some unbelievable memories to release built-up tensions.

Chapter 10

Malakai rides and share laughs with the taxi driver for over thirty minutes as they tour downtown.

The taxi stops at a red light and Malakai notices the long line of beautiful ladies waiting to enter a nightclub.

"Stop right here!"

"Everyone loves *Privée Westlands*. The whole scene is impeccable but if you really want to enjoy yourself check out the rooftop terrace," the driver recommends.

"You can let me out," Malakai admits.

He pays him and stands behind two dark tone ladies and listens to them complain about the entrance line.

I hope trouble don't find me tonight because the one in the red dress could get this dick if I wasn't married.

His dick tingles like spiderman senses. He wipes his forehead "Whew, I better find something else to do until I get in the club."

He recites poetry in his head until a deep voice interrupts his verse. "Next, please."

"Which way leads to the terrace?" Malakai asks.

The bouncer directs, "Make an immediate left passed the bar and the elevators will be down the hall."

"Thank you."

Malakai bobs his head to the music on his way to the rooftop. The elevator door opens and reveals a utopian scene. There is a floating bar in a jacuzzi and the servers wear lingerie and heels.

"Damn the taxi driver was right. This place is amazing."

He sits on a sofa, vibe with the ambiance, and wishes he would have come sooner.

A yellow skin, flat stomach cocktail waitress approaches. "May I take your order?" she asks flashing a gorgeous smile.

'Yes, please bring me a bottle of your finest wine."

"Sure, will there be anything else?"

"Not at this moment."

Her booty cheeks jiggle to the bar and his eyes trail every step. Ladies with diverse nationalities are in the jacuzzi and removing their tops.

"Damn, can this place get any better? The women ratio is double compared to the men. They better be glad this dick is saved. May God be the glory," he praises.

"Good Evening Sir, here's your *Pinotage*. It's a combination of sun-kissed blackberry and black cherry flavors, roasted herbs and a hint of smoke," she describes.

"Are you sure you're not describing juices from the finest woman," he flirts.

She winks, "You never know."

"How much is my tab?"

She steps to the side and waves her hand at the gorgeous ladies. "Mmm, it appears you have new friends because they were checking you out when you stepped out the elevators. They paid your tab."

He pops the bottle, pours a glass, and salutes them.

"This taste like sweet pussy."

"I told you it was mouthwatering."

He reaches into his pocket and pulls out some money. "This is for you and send the other half to the lovely ladies for their gratitude," he offers.

He closes his eyes and embraces the music. He soaks deeper in his chair to forget about the argument. The breeze pushes through and relaxes him more as the DJ mix a few more songs.

"You have some sexy ass lips," a female voice compliments.

He opens his eyes and the ladies from the bar are standing in front of him.

She yanks him out the chair and on the dance floor. The other woman trails behind and sways her body to the music.

The woman in the front bends over and shakes her ass while running her fingers through her hair. The other woman slips her hand over his shoulder and plays with his nipples.

Dancing is an art form, I can do this. It's not like we're going to fuck later.

He cuffs the woman's leg in the air, pulls her close and grinds his crotch between her thighs.

Their dance attracts a crowd and the audience cheer. The woman in the front spins around and rips his shirt open. She pushes him to the ground and hovers over him. "Don't fucking move, you will love what's about to happen," she whispers.

She slaps fives with the other female and pumps up the crowd while skipping in a circle.

The DJ changes the songs to something a little harder and destructive. Malakai could have gone home but his adventurous side craves a new thrill.

She takes off her shirt and whips it in the air before draping it over his face. She performs a somersault and lands perfectly on his dick. She snatches the shirt away, chokes his neck and bounces on his chest.

The crowd claps and toss money on the floor.

Malakai loves the abuse and wants more.

She yanks his hair, slaps his face, and pulls down his pants.

Before she could get too wild, the other female snatches her back. "My turn," she says.

She lifts her shirt and gives him a face full of titties. Her nipples are close enough for him to bite but he keeps his tongue glued to his mouth.

She stands and the other female slides her a chair.

Is this woman going to beat me with this?

She jumps off it, spreads her legs, and her weight explodes on his dick.

"Oh Shit!" He shouts.

She assists him from the ground. "Thanks for joining our act tonight."

"No, thank you for inviting me."

"Anytime, besides you stood out like a sore thumb and we wanted to show you how we party."

"I'm convinced you all are wild as hell, but I loved it." He extends his hands. "By the way, my name is Malakai."

She slaps his hands away. "My pussy has been in your face all night. You better give me a hug."

He laughs, wraps his arms around her waist, and twirls her around.

"Okay, Mr. Excitement, you can put me down."

"My name is Ashanti, and this is my friend Monifa."

He kisses their hands. "It's a pleasure to meet you two. You are welcome to join me if you not busy."

"Sure, why not."

"Great, follow me and I'll show you what this mouth does."

"Umm, what it do boo," Ashanti coos.

"You'll see, but first we need more drinks."

He signals his favorite waitress and escorts the ladies to his sofa and entice their mind with spoken word.

Chapter 11

The morning sunrise erases the stars and fun from last night.

Malakai leaves the club with great memories and a faithful dick. The city is quiet except for a few early go-getters traveling to their workplace.

He whistles for a cab. The driver from last night pulls up. "Hey buddy, where are you going?"

"Please take me to the Villas and could you get me there faster than usual?"

"I know a few shortcuts, buckle your seatbelt."

The driver accelerates, cut a quick left, and speeds down the alley.

He speaks calmly but drives reckless through traffic. "Did you enjoy the rooftop?"

"Did I? Man, it was the best time I had since my daughter's birth."

Ahead of them in the middle of the road is a woman pushing a shopping cart.

"Yo! Watch her," Malakai yells.

The driver toots his horn and swerves around, "Get your ass out the road."

"I always tell her it's some dangerous drivers out here."

Malakai arches his eyebrow. "Yeah, you are the one she should fear most," he mumbles.

The last few miles were less frightening, and the driver arrived early as requested.

Malakai jumps from the seat, opens the door, and toss a wad of cash to the driver.

"What's all the money for?"

"So, your ass can buy a new license," he jokes.

The driver honks the horn. "See you later my brother," he waves and speeds away.

He enters the house and doesn't hear a sound. *Good, I didn't want to hear Asperilla mouth.*

He tiptoes and peeps in Graciana's crib. "Girl, do you ever sleep?"

He retrieves her from the crib. "Let's go outside before your mother wakes up."

"It's amazing how you've grown since we've been here. I'm sure your mother will use me as an example when you become a lady and ask why men cheat. Hopefully, you will never have to experience infidelity in your life."

⚜ ⚜ ⚜ ⚜ ⚜ ⚜ ⚜ ⚜ ⚜ ⚜ ⚜

Asperilla kicks the covers and jumps out the bed.

"Yes, I'm going home, and nothing can stop me," she shouts.

"Rise and Shine Graciana," she sings.

"What the fuck! Malakai do you have Graciana?"

"Malakai, do you have her?" She yells.

She runs to the back and finds them on the patio sleeping peacefully. She slides her hair over her ear. "Thank God! Malakai wake up! You lucky you are holding her, or I would have beat your ass."

"Wow! I must have dozed off."

"That's what happens when you hang out all night with bitches."

"Whatever, I am perfect gentlemen," he proclaims.

"Give her to me and pack our clothes."

She walks through the house and he follows behind her.

"Would you like some breakfast before we go?"

"No, I can eat on the plane."

"Are you sure, because I can flip your favorite pecan waffles?"

"Stop trying to butter me up. You know you fucked up last night."

"Yeah, I know. I promise to do better with communication."

"You and every man on the planet," she responds.

"I love you, Asperilla Valdez. I love you so much, I was happy to drop my last name for yours when we got married," he brags.

She ignores Malakai's statement and plays with Graciana foot. Your father is a retard. Can you say Re-Re?"

Asperilla takes her to the back room and dresses her for the flight.

She snatches her cell phone and it displays 10:00 am. "Malakai, hurry the hell up," she shouts.

He walks over, slides his hand around her waist, and kiss her neck. "Why are you angry all the time?"

"Because I married your black ass."

"You love my black ass."

"Move Malakai, I'm tired and ready to go."

Malakai senses the pain in her voice and leaves her alone to pack the clothes as requested.

He moves nonstop for the next hour, double check the rooms and rolls the luggage outside. "Whew! Damn, we must stop buying so much shit when we are on vacation."

Malakai found the housekeepers and paid them a bonus. "Thanks for being awesome to our family. This won't be the last time we visit."

As he chats with them, the personal driver beeps the horn.

"Well, I believe my time is up. Stay blessed."

"Sir, I can place your bags in the trunk," driver mention.

"Thank you."

"Asperilla, are you sure you have everything?"

"I'm positive baby."

Damn, she calls me baby. Maybe she's not mad at me anymore.

Malakai knew she wouldn't stay mad at him for long, but why rush home knowing Corbin wants them dead. He shakes his head in disgust. "Fuck it! Florida, here we go," he sighs.

He stares out the window one last time before the car disappears down the hill.

"God be with us." He silently prays.

Chapter 12

Every week Corbin visits the home he purchased for Nikki. He inserts the key, turns the knob, and enters the lonely atmosphere. He kept special photos from their dates throughout the house and his favorite one is the downtown carriage ride photo hanging over the fireplace.

His heart sinks as he reminiscence on the countless times they made love on the sofa.

"Nikki, there will never be another woman to take your place," he promises.

He walks to the pool house and playback their last dreadful encounter before she disappeared.

Nikki pulls her fingers out her pussy, clamps and gobbles Corbin's dick in her mouth. Stroking and sucking him deeper down her throat.

"Ahh ahh ahh fuck!"

His moans are music to Nikki's ears.

Corbin ass smacks against the pavement and anticipates the eruption of fireworks to fill her mouth.

Cum shoots like a geyser. Nikki runs her tongue across his head, licking the tip, and chop down with her teeth.

He knew she didn't mean to hurt him. He wanted to assist her with stronger medications to prevent her bipolar outbreaks.

He picks up the patio chair and throws it in the water.

"Fuck you Malakai!" He screams.

He wipes the tears from his eyes, "I'm sorry Nikki, so sorry baby, please forgive me. I wanted us to get married and have a few babies. I wanted to spend every morning washing your pain with my love. My opportunity is over but Malakai and Asperilla won't have a fairytale ending."

He walks back in the house, collects a few pictures and storms out the door. He scrolls through his contact and calls the demolition team. Tomorrow, go to Nikki's house, pack my prized possessions, and level that bitch to the ground. I never want to see it again."

Corbin turns the music on in the car and realizes he needs a temporary flame just someone to share a few kisses or a romantic evening.

"Susan is too easy, I need a challenge and it's time Ayanna realizes what a gentleman can do for her."

She hasn't shared her story, but I will make her break.

He activates the blue tooth. "Call Ayanna."

She answers after the third ring, "Good Afternoon, Mr. Lancaster."

"No need for business this evening. Please call me Corbin," he suggests.

Ayanna becomes quiet on the phone and Corbin dives into the conversation. "We have been working nonstop for a minute. If you are free tonight, will you accompany me for dinner and dancing?"

He never has a problem with ladies, but he never knows what to expect with a woman who was created in Malakai's stable.

He listens to her breath through the phone and with a quick sigh she responds, "Yes."

"Eight o'clock?"

"Yes," he agrees.

"Be early or stay your ass at home."

"I'll make sure I'm extra early."

'I'll text you the address."

"I need to find something sexy to wear so get off my phone."

Corbin tosses the phone on the passenger seat and rides until he arrives at *Channelside Bay Plaza*.

He doesn't normally participate in the city activities due to his work as a DA, but a change of scenery will do some justice.

He parks his car and conducts his own personal tour. He explores the local market and chats with strangers.

The sunrays beam on his skin and music blasts from inside the club venue.

A lovely woman on roller blades passes him in her workout shorts and halter top. Once she passes by, he turns his head to appreciate her plump figure.

She skates a few more feet before slowing down and circling back his way.

"Good afternoon."

"Yes, the afternoon is very good especially since you made a U-turn."

"I'm not sure how you like to spend your evening but if you want Tampa's best experience then visit Love Divine."

She hands him a flyer, kisses his cheek, and skates away.

Corbin flips the flyer over and observes the graphics. "Hmm, looks like an intimate place to meet gorgeous women."

He will make his presence known in the venue soon but not today. He tucks the flyer in his pants and explores another block before heading home to prepare for his date.

Chapter 13

Ayanna clothes are scattered around the room. She takes a step back and can't believe the mess.

"Hell, I can't believe I'm going through this trouble for Corbin's punk ass."

She scratches her head one final time before deciding to go Afrocentric. She takes the Ghanaian print cocktail dress off the hanger.

She flashes a naughty smile. "Yes, this will do perfectly. Since he loves dominant black women, I'll ride his face back to the Motherland."

She glances at the clock and it displays 7:00 pm. "Oh my, where has the time went?" She questions.

She runs to the bathroom and retrieves her *Fenty* Beauty makeup kit. She lies everything on the counter while the water heats up. The steam rise and fogs up the mirror.

She strips naked, enters the shower and relaxes, "Ummm this feels so good."

She seduces herself while washing her skin and hair. She quickly fantasizes everything she would do if Corbin plays his cards right.

After the shower, she wraps her hair and applies her makeup then the doorbell rings.

She doesn't have visitors, so she knows he has arrived early as requested. She opens the door, places her hand over her heart and gasp for air. "Oh, my godness," she screams.

A gigantic stuff puppy, card, and roses sit outside. She snatches the card and reads the inscription.

"Tonight, let's turn back time and have a romantic puppy love evening

Signed your future everything.

Corbin."

She has never met a man who's powerful and corny, but his surprise leaves a tingle in her pussy.

She smiles and brings the gift inside and place it in the living room.

Her phone rings. She throws her hands in the air. "What now. I'm never going to get dress."

"Ayanna?"

"Yes."

"I want you to know I'm patient, take your time. When you are finished; call me and I'll escort you to the car."

"Impressive, you may be a gentleman after all."

"You haven't seen anything yet."

Ayanna response was cut short by the dial tone. "What the hell?"

Did this man hang up in my face? She'll deal with him later. She slips on her clothes and finishes her hair.

"Damn you are one fine bitch," she admits. She imagine the mirror replying, "ATL's finest."

She grabs her purse and dials his number. "Mr. Lancaster, your Queen awaits."

Minutes later there's a knock on the door and she opens to Corbin standing holding a pear shape diamond pendant.

"I believe this will compliment your dress."

She looks at her attire from head to toe and is shocked. "You are really scaring me but I'm woman enough to handle it," she responds.

She spins around and he slides the necklace around her neck. He kisses her shoulder. "Let's make this a night to remember forever."

He escorts her to the car and showcases his expertise as a man with superior manners.

She only accepted his invitation because she was bored. *"What he won't know won't hurt him,"* she chuckles to herself.

Corbin places his hand on her thigh. She jumps and hollers, "Oh shit, you startled me."

"Ayanna, you are safe. Relax."

"Yes, my mind was somewhere else."

"Was it on me?"

She smiles and responds, "Hell no."

"It's ok, it will be later."

"Where are we going anyway?"

He licks his lips and says, "I'm taking my angel back to heaven tonight."

She loved the line but wanted to play hard. She shrugs her shoulder and responds, "Whatever."

"Where's your driver?"

"I'm independent at times Ayanna besides a driver couldn't satisfy my need for speed in a *2018 Pagani Huayra Roadster*. It is equipped for me and you only."

"Corbin, you are humorous when you are outside your office."

"Thank you."

They drive to a familiar place and Ayanna tilts her head and her smiles turn to a frown.

"What's up with the facial expression?"

"I thought we were going somewhere I haven't been before."

"You have never been here before."

"Yes, I have; numerous times."

"Maybe, but you haven't been here with Corbin Lancaster."

He leaps out the car, runs around, and open her door. "Step this way Madam," he escorts.

She extends her hands, and he plants his soft lips on her knuckles. "Ummm… you taste incredible."

He interlocks his hands between hers and leads her to the ramp; lifts her in the air and gently place her in the boat. It has a bar table with champagne, cushion love sofa, flat screen TVs, and fruit trays.

"Wow! Who would have thought this little boat would have accessories like this?"

He powers on the radio and the song *High* by *Ledisi* plays through the surround sound.

She slips off her heels, relaxes on the sofa, and grooves to the song. "That's my shit right there," she claims snapping her fingers.

He navigates the boat through the Bay, passing the art museum, and restaurants before docking at the Marriott hotel.

"Let's drink and count stars until the morning comes," he suggests.

She grins shyly but her inner freak says, *"How about you count these nuts in your mouth."*

He pours the wine, plops in a juicy strawberry, stirs it with his index finger, and trace her lips.

"Umm. Corbin, you better stop fucking with me before you drown out here and I'm not talking about the water."

"Drowning in you is better than living tomorrow without you."

Ayanna sits the glass down and repositions herself. "Corbin let's cut the small talk. What do you want from me?"

"Everything you have to offer."

"I'm damaged goods."

"To who?"

"You don't know anything about my wicked past. I have slept- "

He lifts his finger. "Hush, I don't care," he interrupts.

"You aren't the only person carrying pain around. We all are seeking closure and healing," he admits.

He retrieves some candles from the cabinet and romanticizes the chemistry between them. He drops to his knees and pushes her dress higher. He kisses her kneecaps and rubs her inner thighs.

He stares into her eyes and asks, "Ayanna, do you want me?"

She wanted him from the moment he asked her on a date. She wanted to say, "take me," but her words didn't come out.

He appreciates her silence and knows it is time to make his move and conquer her orgasms.

He presses his fingers into her skin and massages deeper.

She gasps and moans. The way she exhales his name is like a calm wind blowing over the ocean.

He slides his hands higher, cups them under her ass, and pinches her cheeks.

She arches her back, allowing him to slide her thong down to her ankles.

He lifts her foot, sucks her toes, and slides the thong off. He sniffs and tastes her thong before shoving them in his pocket.

He assists taking off her dress and dives between her thighs. He swirls his fingers over her lips and squeezes her clit until her juice drops like tears.

She lusts for a hard fuck but appreciates his sexual mannerism. He takes his time creating a mind-blowing experience to cherish.

He spreads her lips wider, swipes from the bottom, and runs his tongue over her clitoris.

"White boy has oral rhythm," she thinks to herself and pulls his head closer.

He slurps and clamps softly with his teeth, grinds her pussy lips, release, and blow his fresh breath inside.

She exhales and whines over his face. "Aww, you going to make me fall in love with your mouth."

He penetrates her with his fingers, reaches for the wine, and pour some on her navel. He sucks her goblet and finger-fuck her until his veins pop in his forearm.

He returns to her juicy pit, flickering his tongue, and inserting another finger.

"Cum on my face," he whispers.

She crosses her ankles around his neck and thrusts her hips forward. He devours her wetness, grunting harder as she pulls his mouth and nose inside.

"Do you love eating me?"

He lifts his head for air. "Feed me more."

She greedily obliges by stretching her hands around his head and yanking his face to meet her drenched lips.

She throws her head back glazing at the stars. "Oh shit! Eat this pussy baby," she shouts.

He mumbles a few words she cannot make out or care to understand. He bends her legs behind her head while sucking harder and penetrating his fingers deeper than before. He sits her on his face. She reaches for the handrails behind the sofa and recoils her ass and twirls her hips as she grinds down.

He licks stronger and faster as he slurps and bites on her clit.

"Keep going baby cum will be all over your sexy face."

She groans and continues to ride. He increases his technique and latches on her pussy like a Pitbull.

Her body twitches from the pulsating orgasm birthing inside. "Ewww baby, here I… here I…"

Her breathing increases as he eats through her soul. She rides and rides harder as her orgasm explodes and soak his shirt.

He stops but penetrates her with his fingers as she squirts over his arm.

"Shit! Shit!"

Her body shivers and she rattles the handrails praying he will stop working magic with his fingers.

"Stop, please stop."

"You sure you want this to end."

"Yes baby, please," she pleads.

He frees his fingers and sucks on her juices.

She places her hands between her thighs and smiles. "Damn, you can eat pussy," she congratulates.

"I could have eaten you all night."

She waves her index finger. "Come here."

She unzips his pants, pulls his dick out, and shoves it in her mouth.

She jerks and twists, gobbling his meat, and deep throating his existence.

"Whoa! What the fuck, I never had a woman to do this," he proclaims.

He was ready to cum while eating her pussy and now he won't hold his nut too long.

He grabs her hair and fucks her mouth with violent strokes. She loves a good mouth beating and takes the thrusts with pleasure

"Oh, Ayanna."

She grabs his ass and forces him to fuck her harder.

He snatches her head and their movements are in sync.

"Ahhh Shit!" He yells.

He thrusts and releases his nut and she drinks it down like H2O.

He falls on the sofa and closes his eyes. "Damn, your head game is magnificent. I wasn't expecting you to perform miracles."

She plays with his dick. "Are you ok?"

"Yes, give me a moment."

She smiles and cuddles next to him. "Take your time, we have all night to count the stars," she reminds him and continues to stroke his dick.

Chapter 14

Malakai and Asperilla have secretly been home for a week with no disturbances from the outside world. She enjoys the family time but the flirtation for excitement is calling her name.

'Malakai, I have been Mother Teresa far too long. I'm going out tonight."

He bounces his daughter on his knees and nonchalantly says, "Okay, be careful."

The chimes from the outside video camera alerted an incoming vehicle at the gate.

"Are you expecting company?" He asks.

"Not today."

Asperilla press the intercom, "May I help you?"

"Quit playing games and let us in," Jaz responds.

"Looks like your welcoming party is here. You knew damn well you were going out before you mention it with your sneaky ass."

She twists her fingers in her hair, runs over and gives him a kiss. "Yes, I knew. When I come back, I'll give you a night on the town too."

She rushes upstairs and without looking back she hollers, "Let them in while I change."

He places the baby in the crib and opens the front door. "Aww shit its *Heckle and Jeckle*," he announces.

"It's good to see you too," Jaz answers.

Cherry rushes through, almost knocking him down as she races to see Graciana. "Get out the way."

She covers her face with kisses.

"Quit kissing her. I don't know where your mouth has been," he lectures.

"No damn where because you want us to keep a low-profile like your boring ass. I need some dick in my life," Jaz interjects.

"No one is stopping you from fucking, I'm sure it's plenty of niggas out there you can slob on," he jokes.

"Yeah, I know but the nut is better when cash is involved."

He says while shaking his head, "There is something wrong with you."

The doorbell rings. "Who else is with you bitches?"

Jaz and Cherry didn't respond. He squints his eye through the peephole and didn't see anyone. He grabs his gun under the chair, flips the switch to fire, swings the door, and finds Ayanna standing there.

"You were about to eat some bullets. Why the fuck are you sneaking around?"

"I was in the SUV the whole time. I came to surprise Asperilla along with the girls."

Ayanna walks in and snaps her fingers in the air. "Ladies, the original dick drainers are reunited."

He reminisces on the days they fed this city the best pussy known to man.

"Malakai, when is our next erotic show?" Jaz asks.

"The last time you were supposed to demonstrate not tug on my dick for real. I'll take a rain check on your crazy ass."

He pulls Ayanna to the side to avoid the other ladies from hearing their conversation. "Do you have Corbin's financial records?"

"I should have them by next week. He keeps secure paperwork locked inside a safe under his desk. I probably could get it sooner, but Ms. Drummond's nosy ass is always around."

"What made you come back so soon? I wasn't expecting y'all for another month until Cherry called and said Asperilla invited us out for a ladies' night."

"Yeah, it wasn't my idea but it's too late now."

Jaz sneaks into the kitchen and brings out a bottle of *Ménage a Trois*. "Watch my new trick!" She shouts.

She opens her mouth and demonstrates how far she could swallow the bottle without choking. She pulls it out, pops the top, and pour it drown her throat. "This Midnight flavor is delicious. Yall want some?"

"Hell naw." Ayanna responds.

"Jaz stay the fuck out my kitchen! Y'all thirsty bitches need to hurry up and leave. Asperilla!" Malakai screams.

"Lower your voice. You are scaring the baby," Cherry advises.

"Ladies I'm ready!!" Asperilla announces.

She stands at the stairwell dressed in a thin crop jacket, halter top, skinny jeans and thigh boots. Her abs are solid, and there wasn't any baby weight.

"Where the hell you think you are going dressed like that?" Malakai asks.

She tosses her hair to the side. "Didn't I tell you it's ladies' night? Don't worry, I'm sure Graciana will enjoy the quality time with you."

"Make sure your ass is home at a decent hour.
"Whatever."

"Ladies, ready?"

She glides down the stairs and kisses Graciana good night. "Mami loves you and make sure you give your father hell. Malakai, her milk is in the refrigerator, her- "

"I got this. You and your sluts have a wonderful evening," he interrupts.

"Fuck you!" Cherry snaps back.

"I love being a slut," Jaz responds.

"Girl, I should have left your ass in Houston, "Ayanna says.

They head out to the door with their belongings to the SUV.

"So, where are you all taking me?" Asperilla asks.

"A place where you can see tits and dicks," Jaz hints.

"Asperilla excuse the freak, you are going to an art gallery," Cherry blurts.

Cherry looks at Jaz, attempts to hide her smile, burst into laughter and says, "Art gallery with dicks by the pounds."

Asperilla smiles. "I really miss you bitches. Thanks for taking me out because I've been cooped up with his ass twenty-four-seven. Pussy Rehab has created a nerve wrecking monster. He's always under me. I'm not used to being smothered. I might let him fuck some side pussy, so he can stay the hell away from me for a while."

Jaz places her head between her legs and whispers, "You hear that Jazzy, there's a God after all."

Everyone in the SUV erupts with laughter.

After the mood settles, Asperilla notices Jaz sipping on some wine. She snatches the bottle from her hand. "Stay out my stash," she warns.

Jaz responds. "Since you are a mother now, I figured you wouldn't miss it," she responds.

"Whatever hoe!"

"I love being a hoe, but you all refer escort."

"Girl, you are the reason why I need a drink," Asperilla responds.

She takes a drink and passes the bottle back to Jaz.

Asperilla notices Ayanna being extra quiet during the drive. "What have you been up to and why are you so distant?"

"I was thinking about my new case. I promise it won't interfere with our night," Ayanna answers.

"I hope not because the secret conversations you and Malakai are having is annoying as hell. Next time, include everyone on the mission."

Cherry turns her head to the back. "What mission?"

"Corbin Lancaster." Asperilla blurts.

Cherry gives Ayanna a double look. "Why are you all fucking with a district attorney?"

"Because they can't let the dead stay buried," Asperilla interrupts. He is stressing about Corbin coming for us and it's worse since I had the baby. Fuck Corbin and Nikki dead ass. I wish he would try some shit. I'm not afraid to go to jail for killing his punk ass," Asperilla rants.

Asperilla leans from her seat and places her hand on Ayanna's shoulder. "Abort your mission and don't bring Corbin or Nikki's name to my doorstep."

"I'm doing a favor for Malakai and I don't work for you anymore," Ayanna reminds her and continues to drive.

Asperilla is seconds away from snatching Ayanna's hair and pulling her into the back seat.

"Ladies let's see what's on the radio," Cherry says.

She flips on the radio and *Trip* by *Ella Mai* calms the mood. Jaz sings the chorus and grinds in the seat.

Asperilla leans back, close her eyes and sings with Jaz.

Ayanna stares at Asperilla through the rearview mirror. "Bitch I can't stand you," she mumbles under her breath.

Chapter 15

The ladies park and venture to the art gallery. The street has a neocentric feeling with music and food.

Jaz takes a deep sniff, "Damn, I pray the aroma is coming from the gallery. I'm hungry as hell," she admits while rubbing her stomach.

Cherry giggles and slaps Jaz ass. "Bitch! You are always hungry. Bring your ass on so we can find a good seat."

They scurry pass security and locate their VIP seats filled with colorful balloons and complimentary bottles.

A waiter approaches wearing a bowtie, black boots, and a Tarzan dick drapes along his inner thigh. 'Welcome to the art gallery, my name is Marcellus your welcoming party.'

Jaz spits in her hand, balls a fist and lubricates his shaft before Cherry snatches her back.

"Can't take your ass anywhere. Act like you have some home training."

"Thanks for introducing your tight grip," he mentions to Jaz with a wink. "If you all need anything tonight… don't hesitate to ask." He turns around displaying his firm ass.

"Damn! You see the muscles in his ass cheeks. I bet he can squat a fucking horse," Jaz shouts.

Cherry pops the bottle and pours everyone a drink. "Asperilla you haven't always been the perfect friend, boss, or sister. You were the biggest asshole to work for, but our life wouldn't be shit without you in it."

They clink the glasses and dance to the music.

Over the next hour, they watch the photographer snap pictures of the nude models as the artist's sketch their vision.

Asperilla knocks on the table while the girls were passing around their fifth shot. "Sorry girls, but I don't drink a lot when I'm outside the house."

"More for me," Jaz mentions and guzzles her shots.

"I should have become a nude model," Jaz mentions.

"What's stopping you?" Cherry asks.

Asperilla throws a stack on the table, "Liberate yourself and set your mind free."

"Oh, you think I won't."

Cherry clanks her glass over the table and chants, "Bet you won't, I bet you won't."

"Fuck ya'll, I ain't never scared."

She removes her clothes, slips on her heels and dances her way to center stage.

"I was only joking," Cherry proclaims.

"Pull your lips back and show them the wet *Mona Lisa*," Asperilla screams from the VIP section.

Jaz acknowledges Asperilla request by pumping her fist in the air before a gentleman assists her on stage.

Cherry knew tonight's outing would be weird between Asperilla and Ayanna. She attempts to play peacemaker between them. "Ayanna, how's life in ATL?'

"It's wonderful but not the same adventure as Tampa."

"Stick around a little longer. I'm sure Asperilla will provide us some pleasure," Cherry hints.

"I could use a wild night."

"You think you can keep up. I would hate for you to catch a cramp on your first outing," Asperilla jokes.

"Oh, I can hang with the best. You're the one on maternity leave…forever," Ayanna responds. "Let's see who can pull the most phone numbers in here."

"These young men aren't interested in cougar pussy. Sit ya'll asses down," Cherry says.

Ayanna pours another shot and throws it back. "Asperilla I bet you a G, I can get more numbers than you in five minutes," she challenges.

"Ayanna, you sure you want to do this?" Asperilla asks. "Cherry, grab Jaz to help us count."

Ayanna crosses her legs and flips her middle finger in Asperilla's face.

She grabs Ayanna's hair, yanks her over and pierces her bottom lips with her teeth. She releases and pushes her head away. "Why are you really here?"

"I don't want to be, but Malakai needed my service. Unlike you."

Asperilla laughs and responds, "Bitch, sending you to Atlanta was great. You graduated law school and now you are an assistant district attorney."

"Whatever Asperilla, don't worry I won't interrupt your perfect life. I will be leaving shortly."

"Your mouth is becoming disrespectful. I should have whooped your ass in the car earlier. Don't forget you wasn't shit before me," Asperilla reminds her and calms down once Jaz and Cherry arrives.

"Did ya'll see the attention I was getting," Jaz asks slipping on her dress. "They fucking love me. I believe I have a new hustle."

"Cherry, we are ready for this phone number challenge," Asperilla announces.

"Okay, each cell has a number, memorize yours, and have the guy text his number to it. The DJ will spin one track while you all collect as many numbers before the song ends," Cherry explains.

Ayanna walk passed Asperilla and scroll to the floor. Asperilla follows in pursuit and stops at the booth to scroll through his track lists.

The DJ smiles and nods his head. He scratches the mixer and plays *Twerk* by *City Girls*.

Asperilla rocks her head, jiggle her hips toward her first number.

Ayanna dances on some local rappers and professional athletes.

Asperilla dances between some fellas and ladies.

She twerks on one lucky guy. "Gimmie your phone," she whispers.

She grinds her ass into his crotch and he happily obliges. His erection builds as she dances. She pops her ass and texts multiple contacts to her phone until the DJ finishes the track.

She flips him the phone, "Stop by our VIP in five minutes."

Ayanna marches from the floor with a gigantic smile on her face from the numbers she secured from the men. "Where's Asperilla?"

"Here I go." She responds walking from behind.

"Cherry do the honors," Asperilla says.

Cherry flips the phone over, displaying all the texts. Cherry counts the numbers and reveals the winner is Asperilla.

Ayanna snatches the phones from her hands. "I'm sure her ass cheated."

"Stop hating, you have been out the game too long." Asperilla reminds her by blowing on her knuckles and wiping her shirt.

"You were in their ears whispering your cell number one by one. That's a great way if you were looking for a date but I snatched my numbers from one guy," Asperilla admits

"His contacts were probably coworkers or bitches he is fucking. I don't give a fuck, remember a tight ass distracts a nigga always," Asperilla reveals. "Don't sleep on me because I have a baby. I am the champion and you are the loser."

Ayanna hates losing and produces a fake smile to keep the tension away.

Asperilla smiles and winks at her. "I have a second-place constellation prize."

"What tricks do you have up your sleeves now?"

Asperilla nods her head and the sexy guy she danced with earlier makes his way over.

Stepping in their VIP section is a 6'2 Chocolate God with locs falling down his back.

"I didn't catch your name earlier," Asperilla suggests.

He blushes for a second and flashes his pearly white teeth. He responds, "Antonio," in a New York accent.

"This is Cherry, Jaz, and Ayanna," she introduces.

"Good Evening ladies, thanks for the invitation."

"Antonio, Ayanna lost a contest and I'm wondering if you can change her facial expression for one night."

"Yeah, she needs her back broken," Jaz chimes in.

"Can you provide hard strokes and choke service?" Asperilla asks.

"What the fuck?" Ayanna shouts.

"You asked for a wild night and this is a perfect way to jumpstart your pussy meter."

"Ahem, what about me?" Jaz interjects.

Asperilla snaps her fingers and Marcellus strolls over. "Marcellus and Antonio, you are about to experience a pussy dripping utopia. Are you ready to taste wisdom?" Asperilla asks.

They grin and nod.

"Cherry take me home because all this sex talk has me ready to mount my husband's face."

Asperilla and Cherry exits the art gallery. "Are you sure they will be ok?"

"Certainly, plus I know them. They used to be regular clients before we scaled back the business. By the way, how is your fiancé?" Asperilla questions.

"We are preparing for our wedding. Would you like to be my maid of honor?"

"Gladly."

"I'm happy you found someone. You deserve it."

Cherry unlocks the car and drive down the road.

"Are you and Ayanna good?"

"Wild history but we will be alright."

"*History I never want to share with Malakai,*" she mutters to herself.

Chapter 16

Ayanna cell buzzes on the nightstand as her face is buried in the pillow. She ignores it. An hour later, it rings again. She reaches and answers, "Corbin what the fuck you want this early, it's the damn weekend."

She hangs up, tosses the phone and rolls on Antonio's hard naked body. She usually doesn't entertain a leftover guest, but his dick was thick and convincing. She reaches between his thighs and squeezes his dick causing him to flinch.

"How long was I sleeping?" He asks while rubbing his eyes.

"Since I rode your last nut out," she coos.

"Shit! I wasn't expecting all those tricks. My dick is sore as fuck. I believe you rode the skin off."

"You are lucky I didn't suck away your life."

Ayanna gets out the bed, walks to the restroom, and return with towels. "You are welcome to take a shower; the men gel is on the top shelf."

He flashes his sexy grin, "Will I see you again?"

She kisses his forehead and squeezes his dick a second time. "You never know what the universe has in store. Go freshen up and I'll blend my favorite smoothie for to take with you."

She walks to the kitchen, opens her refrigerator, and grabs some mixed fruit. She turns on the TV and watches the morning news.

Antonio walks in and Ayanna wishes she could drink him one last time. "Here's your smoothie."

He sips, lick his lips, and moans, "Umm sweet like your pussy."

"Sure, it is, I sprinkled my juices to give you energy."

"Are you for real?"

She punches him in the arm and jokes. "I'm fucking with you."

He sits the glass on the counter and wraps his arms around her lower back. "Ayanna, thanks for the lovely evening."

"You are welcome. Did you leave my money on the nightstand?"

"What for?"

"Fucking your brains out."

"You are silly and sexy," he compliments.

"I have been told."

She walks him to the door and watches him drive off.

She closes it and returns to the texts, missed calls, and voicemails. "Check your voicemail," one text reads.

Ayanna listens, presses the call swiftly and waits for Corbin to pick up.

"Finally, you decided to answer your phone. I guess you are through sexing your new man."

Ayanna huffs through the phone and responds with a slight attitude. "Corbin let's get one thing straight. You are a wonderful person. Your head game is incredible but I'm a single woman and free to do whom and whatever."

Corbin laughs and responds. "Are you done being a comedian?"

"Yes, I am and making sure you know where we stand."

She calms down and gathers her composure. "How the hell you knew who I was sexing anyway? Fucking stalker," she concludes.

"Baby, I never stalk women. I have a team and they report everything even your ladies' night with Asperilla.

Why didn't you tell me they were back in town? Are you having second thoughts on taking them out?"

"No! I was only gaining her trust."

"Ayanna, my resources are deadly. We shouldn't be arguing. Can you open your front door?"

"Why?"

"Because I want to make things right between us."

Ayanna isn't sure why she's listening to Corbin after he admitted he had her followed. She wants to leave him outside, but she couldn't resist his charm.

She opens the door and he pins her against the wall. "I know you didn't get satisfied and you probably had to do all the work."

She laughs and pushes him away. "You are crazy as hell. Follow me."

She sits at the kitchen counter, power on her laptop, and opens a file displaying Malakai's home.

"You aren't the only one with resources."

She hadn't watched the live feed since she moved to Atlanta. She opens the refrigerator and searches for something to eat because Asperilla and Malakai playing house pisses her off.

"Asperilla bitch ass lied to you. She's never leaving Malakai. Fuck that ugly ass baby too. Kill them all," she thinks to herself.

She snatches the orange juice and gulps it down.

She slams the refrigerator. "Ok, Corbin, I'm ready to finish the plan."

Corbin smiles. "I've been waiting to see this side of you."

He wraps his arms around her. "How about you take a shower and have dinner with me. You can pick anywhere in the world you like to go."

"Anywhere you say?"

"I didn't stutter, did I?"

Ayanna breaks free from his grasps. "Take me to Spain," she yells while running to the shower.

He waited until she disappears and dials Ms. Drummond. "Susan how are you doing this morning?"

"Don't Susan me. You probably at Ayanna's house. I'm sure after you get Malakai you won't need me."

"Why are you acting like that? Do me a favor and contact the team."

"Whose bodies are you disposing this time?"

"No death this time. I ran a license plate number and he's a good candidate for extortion."

"What's his name?"

"Antonio Willis."

"Okay, I have the team conduct a routine traffic stop this week. Will that be all?"

"Yes, I have to get back to Malakai."

"Or Ayanna," she responds.

"I'm working business and besides Malakai is a delicate assignment. We need Ayanna," he confesses.

"Have you decided to kill him?"

"I'm contemplating something scandalous with six figures involved. I will see you soon and you can brief me on Antonio."

"Sure, I'll have the report ready."

"Susan, another thing."

"Yes?"

"Please stop being jealous. There's enough loving for everyone."

"Humph," she answers back and hangs up.

Corbin places his phone in his pocket and drops to his knees outside the bathroom door

Ayanna opens the door and asks. "Corbin, what are you doing?"

"Showing you how a real King serves his Queen," he demonstrates.

He rises and kisses her shoulders. "Hurry and get dressed before we are late for our flight."

She grabs her yoga pants, shirt, and toss a lotion bottle to Corbin. "Mr. Romantic, you can use your hands and caress my soft skin."

"It would be my pleasure."

She leans on the bed and he squeezes the lotion in his palms, rubbing his hands together and massaging her body.

He kisses her belly button. "Get dress baby. I'll make sure to take you shopping when we land in Madrid."

She kisses his lips, jumps from the bed, and throws on her clothes. "Let's go, I'm ready!"

Ayanna rushes outside to the car and jumps in the passenger seat.

"I'm not mad you fucked a side piece. You will soon learn why your life will be half full until you fall in love with the one and only Corbin Lancaster," he boasts.

"You're as arrogant as they come?"

"Damn right."

"Now let's go to Spain, make love, and return to destroy our enemies."

Chapter 17

Malakai creeps through the house like a ninja to avoid waking up Graciana. He kisses Asperilla's shoulder, "If you need me, I'll be on *Bayshore* for an afternoon run."

Asperilla yawn in his face and rolls on her stomach.

"Your ass is too old to be partying and drinking."

He leaves and takes the scenic route. He stretches and warmup before slipping on his headphones. His playlist will keep him motivated throughout the run. He sprints passed baby strollers and group runners.

He ran a few more miles and reaches heavy traffic. He halts as he approaches the block where his nightclub is located. He hasn't been inside, nor has he accepted any calls from Monique.

He removes his headphone, wipes the sweat, and strolls to the entrance. He opens the door and *Bam* by *Jay Z* greets him in the face.

Monique redecorated the top and bottom floor. His gold-plated microphone glisters from a distance; teasing him to initiate wet wordplay. He makes his way to the stage, closes his eyes and massages the microphone's head. He mentally squirts words like cum in the shower.

"Stressful times has taken away her smile and it's up to me to produce days of happiness. She deserves heaven on Earth, a rebirth, appreciate for what she's worth. I want to hold her until time freeze. Now that I have your attention. Did I mention? That I want to create another dimension with your black hole. Searching through milky waves while spinning your rings of Saturn. Going where no man has gone before. Deep Space… Until my mind become weak and erased. God existed in our bedroom and the neighbors

shall hear you, me, we. Shouting Psalms 63:3 because our love is better than life and my lips will glorify you."

Hand clapping interrupts his flow and Monique stands screaming, "Rewind."

"Nah, I'm good; just playing around."

He jumps from the stage and sweeps Monique off her feet. He kisses her cheeks and places her on the ground. "How have you been? I love what you've done with the place."

"Well, you know. What can I say?"

He grabs her hand and says, "Let's have a seat and catch up."

"Malakai, I have work to do."

"I know but there's always time to chat. How's business? Are you having any issues I need to handle?"

"I'm wonderful, the club is amazing, and money is flowing every week. You made me a partner for a reason so enough club talk. How big is Graciana and how's Asperilla?"

"Everyone is fine but truthfully, I wish I stayed in Kenya. It's peaceful, beautiful, and I'm not recognized."

She giggles and responds, "Malakai is finally growing up. Did you graduate from Whore Rehab?"

"Yep. I bought a cap and gown too."

She jokes until his facial expression turns.

"Is something bothering you?"

"Some days I'm paranoid as hell. My gut tells me Corbin is coming to avenge Nikki's death. I want to march in his office and place a bullet between his eyes. If it wasn't for his position as a district attorney, I would have killed him a long time ago."

Monique exhales, "You are carrying heavy shit on your shoulders. Pray and let it go."

"I've been trying but my love for poetry is imbalanced fearing another crazy groupie."

Monique lifts her dress and rubs her hands over the scar from her knife wound. "That crazy bitch left a serious impact. I live with those memories every day, but I also refuse to give my past power over me. You will get passed it. Now get your ass out the club unless you are performing tonight."

"You are right, but an insurance plan isn't a bad thing to have."

"I agree."

"Do me a favor?"

"Sure!"

"The next time you are in my office, please pay close attention to my first poetry album. The title is a name of a friend for you to contact if anything goes wrong."

"Ok, I gotcha."

"Thanks! In the meantime, I'll see if I can rejuvenate my skills on the mic again."

He gives her a hug and jogs the long way back to the shore.

He gets to his car and reminiscence about the things discussed before starting the ignition. He flips down the visor displaying a picture of Asperilla and Graciana from the delivery room. He prays he's not making a mistake on his next decision. He syncs his Bluetooth to the radio. "Ayanna," he announces.

"Hey Malakai, what's good?"

"Let me get to business. Abort the mission with Corbin and return to Atlanta."

"Are you sure?"

"No, but I'm tired of washing my hands in blood. I'm going off the grid forever."

Ayanna senses the seriousness in his voice. She knows if he disappears, Corbin will never find him and might have her killed.

"What about Asperilla, are you sure she will leave?"

"Who gives a fuck what she wants? It's time for a new life. Don't do anything stupid. I'll find a way for you to leave Corbin ranks without suspicion. Ayanna be careful and if you need me don't hesitate to call. I'll be around 24/7."

They terminate the call and he cruises out the city and accelerates down the interstate.

Chapter 18

Ayanna has been ignoring Asperilla calls and texts since Malakai informed her about relocating.

Now his ass wants me to abort the mission, so he can protect his family. "Damn his family!" She yells.

Her phone chimes and the text reads, "Are we hanging out tonight and why aren't you answering your phone?" "*Fuck naw, you backstabbing bitch*! she thinks.

Ayanna calls Corbin instead. He answers on the first ring. "Damn, were you waiting by the phone?"

"I'm telekinetic."

"Whatever, I'm coming over. Text me your address."

"Is everything alright?"

"I'll explain when I get there."

"Okay."

The text came, and she packs an overnight bag. She does a final check to make sure she has everything and drives to Corbin's house. The Causeway traffic is bumper to bumper. She taps her newly manicured nails against the steering wheel pondering wicked ideas to split apart the power couple. She plots a few scenarios, but none life quenching.

She turns on the radio and sings along to a few songs. The traffic breaks and she hopes Corbin has a plan to keep them around longer.

She arrives in the *Sunset Park* and remembers this neighborhood from the rich clients she seduced.

Within minutes the GPS announces, "You have arrived."

She opens her car door, flings her bag over her shoulders, and presses the doorbell.

A butler dressed in a tuxedo opens the door. He bows and returns to his position. "Good day, Ms. Ayanna, may I take your bags?"

She smiles, hands over the bag, and follows him through the house. She passes Corbin's historical artifacts, trophies, and wild game. She runs her fingers down the ferocious lion's tooth as she walks behind the butler.

He leads her downstairs to the recreation room, "Good Afternoon Mr. Lancaster, Mrs. Ayanna is here for your enlightenment."

Corbin plays pool shirtless and focusing on making his final shot with the eight ball. Ayanna watches as the cue sticks slide between his fingers. Her pussy becomes moist by watching the determination on his face. He pulls the stick back, gently knock the white ball against the eight ball. It travels along the table and drops in the top left corner. After making the shot, there was no excitement or celebration. He is calm and free spirited like he was in a room with invisible people.

"Thank you, Thomas. Please take her bag to the guest room."

"Yes Sir, will there be anything else?"

He turns and tips him. "That will be all for today. Thank you for your service."

She arches her eyebrow and gives Corbin a curious look. "Why do you tip if he works for you?"

He smiles before answering. "I love making people feel appreciated. He earns his check and received his monthly salary, but a person will display loyalty once they feel respected."

"I guess."

He places the pool stick on the table. "Okay, Ms. Ayanna, let's discuss why you are stressed."

"What do you think when you see me?"

"I might over analyze your character. I better leave my thoughts to myself."

"No, I want your brutal opinion. You judge people characters all the time."

"But that's my job."

"Consider me no different."

"Alright, if you insist. You are a woman who killed, stole, and sold your body for your own crew. Loyal to the death until something triggers your life on a new path. Honestly, I don't trust you fully, so you need to make me a believer."

"What do you mean, you don't trust me?"

"You were sent to kill me now you are on my team. I'm feeling you, but I need to know if you are someone, I can consider an ally. I'm truly disappointed in you right now."

Her eyes widen and her lip curls. "Why?"

"When you came to see me, it was about taking over my organization and getting rid of Malakai; I was truly impressed. Since you have been hanging with Asperilla, you seem distracted and if you want out, just leave."

She leaps from the chair. "What the fuck are you talking about Corbin?"

"Either we fulfill our plans to destroy them or you get the hell out of my house."

"You men are alike. Are you still upset I fucked Antonio? Yeah, I rode his dick like a horse. Is that what you want to hear Corbin Lancaster? Maybe coming over here was a mistake. I'll gather my things and leave."

He sees the fire in her eyes and teases her harder. "What's stopping you from leaving?"

All the frustration and anger enter the palm of her hands when she slaps his face.

He smiles and rubs it. "Yes, this is the woman I need right now."

She places her hands on her hips. "Stop fucking with me, Corbin!"

He carries her to the recliner. "Straddle me," he commands.

"I'm not fucking your insensitive ass after all that shit."

He drops her on the bed, unbuttons his pants, and slides them to the floor. "You have been fucked over so long until you don't know what love feels like. Allow me to show you. Now, take off your clothes and straddle me. I tasted your pain on the boat and there's more I need you to release. Trust me."

She removes her clothes and pushes him on the bed. "I can't believe I'm doing this."

"Life begins when your happiness comes."

She inserts one finger in her wetness and places it in his mouth.

"Ummm, you taste ready," he moans.

She straddles and eases his dick into her pool. She closes her eyes while gyrating in ecstasy.

"Ayanna," he whispers.

"Yes, Corbin," she moans seductively.

His thrust becomes relief with each stroke. "Tell me about your pain."

She twirls her hips, grips his dick, and releases. "Don't judge me, Corbin, please don't judge me."

She grabs his head and opens her soul to him. She rides his dick and journey to her earlier days as an escort.

"Here's my story. Malakai taught me to never fall in love with a client but there was one who melted my heart. He was the only man I slept with unprotected and paid extra to keep me around. He always vowed to take care of me. I believed every word until I discovered he had a wife and kids after I became pregnant. I was angry, hurt, lost and scorned. I secretly scheduled another visit with him and planted a knife in his chest. I stab him repeatedly, over... over... and over... Blood soaked the sheets, smeared the wall, and I-."

She paused her story, gasps for air, and continues riding.

"I'm listening, don't stop."

She exhales, grinds and contines. "I wasn't sure how he would react to me killing his client, so I called Asperilla. She helped me clean up the evidence and suggested I abort the baby. I listened and we became friends and lovers. We had plans of overthrowing Malakai and taking over the business. Everything changed when he started trusting me more. She found pleasure with Pandora and flaunted it in my face. I ignored the shit and focused on school; until one night she forced me to move back to Atlanta with a broken heart and unfilled promises. My life was perfect there. I was mentally and financially stable with no regrets."

Ayanna claws Corbin's back thinking about her pain she caused.

She leans back, thrusting on his dick, and springs to her normal position on his lap.

"Where was I?"

"You were secure in your success," Corbin mentions.

"Yeah, things were well until I found out about the pregnancy. Now I want Asperilla to experience the death of a child too."

She smiles, closes her eyes and rides faster.

"That's right baby releases all your anger."

He thrusts deeper while her ass smacks against his thighs every time she lands.

"Do you want your revenge?"

She pulls his hair and screams, "I want it, I want it like this nut."

Her clit twitches as she leans down and bite Corbin's earlobe. She clamps tighter and he moans, "Aww shit."

Her cum electrifies her soul as she jerks for the final time and rolls onto the floor.

He runs his fingers across her skin and ask, "Your sex drive escalated into overdrive. Are you ok?"

She kisses his cheek, "Never better, I'm ready to get even with my old crew. Corbin?"

"Yes baby."

"Thank you for the release."

"Anytime."

"I believe I have a little bit of pain on my clit. Do you think you can suck the last drop?"

"Gladly," he responds and crawls between her legs.

She uses her thighs like vise grips and clamps his head as he sucks and eats her pussy.

"Umm, our revenge will cum like my second one."

She blocks out all her pain by appreciating his undivided attention and senses her plan being fulfilled.

Chapter 19

After ignoring Asperilla for a week, Ayanna is ready to listen to her bullshit.

She dials her number and Asperilla wastes no time running her smart mouth.

"Hoe! Where have you been?"

"Wow, you were never taught to say hello? You do know I don't work for you anymore."

"Bitch! You will always work for me considering you have been ignoring my calls. What the fuck you do to Malakai?"

"What do you mean?"

Asperilla chuckles, "I swear I'm trying to be a better woman, but you are going to catch these hands. You were here to do a mission and return to Atlanta. I guess your plan failed because he wants to go off the grid and drag me with him."

"Let me explain."

"I'm listening."

"He had a change of heart and asked me to abort the mission."

"I wish you never came back to Tampa. Thanks for fucking up my world again."

"Your world, what about- "

"Don't go there, Ayanna. I protected you," Asperilla interrupts. "I apologize if you feel wronged, but you can't keep blaming me for the past."

"The hell I can't," Ayanna thinks.

"I'm not fighting with you today. Matter of fact, I'm inviting you to a farewell party at the club."

It is moments before Ayanna responds, "I'll be there."

Asperilla hangs up the phone and smacks her lips when Malakai walks in. He bypasses her, drinks his water from the refrigerator, and toss it in the recycle bin.

He understands the anger on her face and tries to console her. "Baby, I love you."

She turns her back and responds, "Sure, you do."

He reaches his hands around her waist and kisses her neck.

"Stop that shit! Dick cannot cure everything."

"What the fuck are you talking about?"

"You know what the fuck I mean. I'll go to your whack party but Graciana and I aren't leaving Tampa."

"Yes, the fuck you are," he screams while slamming his fist on the counter.

The doorbell rings ending the heated discussion.

She spins around and sings, "Ding-Dong, the witch is dead."

"You are expecting company?"

"Yep, my delivery dick," she responds sarcastically.

"Asperilla, get the door before I throw you out."

"Wow! Now, we are getting somewhere maybe the old Malakai does exist."

She trots through the kitchen and opens the door. "Isabella, welcome back,"

She jumps in Asperilla's arms and kisses her cheek. "I'm happy to be back. I'm shocked your crazy aunt allowed me to return. You know she is extra protective and shit."

"Girl, I already know. Trust me, I've been there."

"Follow me to the day room so you can see how big Graciana is now."

"Why is Isabella here?"

Asperilla shakes her head, "Malakai, you can't protect the world. Go write a poem or do something constructive. This has been a stressful week and I'm tired of fighting with you."

She grabs Isabella's hand and drags her away.

He enters the bedroom, turns on the shower and waits for the water to heat up. "Which poem do I want to perform," he ponders while staring in the mirror.

He never does anything in advance and the club doesn't know he's coming. He loves sneaking up on them and this showcase will be one for the ages.

Asperilla words flow through his head, *"Where is the old Malakai?"*

He closes his eyes, inhales, and exhales, "Tonight, the whole city will see me in full view."

His erection rises from the thought of poetry and veins tighten along his shaft. "Are ready to slay?" He asked while clutching it inside his fist.

He lifts and makes it nod, "Yes."

He steps in the shower, drops his head, and thinks about an erotic poem. Once he locates one from the vault. He tests the words on himself. Licking his hand and massaging his dick with his saliva. He presses his palm against the wall and slow stroke until he spits the first verse.

"She wants a seductive stroke. One that cuts off her oxygen flow. Leaving her soul paralyzed after I swing it between her thighs. Attacking her brain, until she forgets her name."

He strokes his dick faster, breathing heavier as he recites his piece. The tingling in his head feels wonderful. He beat his fist against the wall.

"My seductive strokes come in all dimension and when the dick is tired my tongue becomes an extra extension to

make you tap out to my sexual submission. I just don't deliver ordinary strokes. I row strokes like your pussy is a sinking boat. I row and row until you can't take it any mo."

"Fuck this poem," he grunts.

He flops to the shower base and thrusts his dick through his hands. Water flashes his face as he lifts his hips in the air and jacks his dick faster and faster. "Oh shit."

His mind drifts to Asperilla riding his dick while he fingers her ass. "Ride my dick bitch. Yea, just like that. Drain this dick, you nasty muthafucker. Ahh yeah, cum for daddy."

The first load shoots and lands under his Adam's apple. The second loads erupt on his nipples amazed at his artwork. He plays and tastes his masterpiece until the shower door swings open.

"What the fuck are you doing?" Asperilla asks.

"I'm rejuvenating myself for later."

"Good me too," she answers and removes her clothes. "Rinse off and beat this pussy."

"You not mad at me?"

"Hell, yeah but my pussy loves you."

He extends his hand and she slaps it away. "Change of plans." She pushes him down and sits on his face. "Eat this pussy first since you like cumming without me," she orders.

He is super delighted and thankful for the surprise. She brutalizes his face and he gulps her sweet juices. He slaps her ass to make her ride harder. She bronco his face as requested, playing with her nipples as he delivers the best head.

"What a way to start the morning. Tonight will be even better."

Chapter 20

Malakai presses the automatic window to eye level. The money scent lingers in the air as they pass the inpatient people standing in general admission.

He didn't want to be seen but it's hard to keep a secret about his triumphant return to Love Divine.

Tampa elites are driving to the curb in their finest cars, and expensive attire. He's impressed with the turnout and will make sure to thank Monique for her marketing skills.

The driver pulls in the alley and they enter through the rear door.

The original crew is holding a banner with the words "Welcome Back Poet" printed in bold gold letters.

"Don't make me cry before the show. We have been through a lot together and I want to-."

"Malakai, are you getting sensitive?" Jaz blurts.

"Fuck no! I'm feeling like my old self. I appreciate and love you all. Allow me to express my gratitude."

He presses send on his phone and a text message with an off-shore account number appears on everyone phone.

Jaz was the first one to tap her key and her eyes sparkle like a diamond.

She jumps in his arms. "You gave me half a mill. Oh shit! My pussy is rejoicing."

"Move Bitch! Get out the way," Cherry jokes while pushing Jaz.

Cherry squeezes him tightly, "I know what this is for and thank you," she whispers.

"I'll check mine later. I don't want y'all nosey asses in my business," Ayanna states with a nonchalant attitude.

"Money ain't everything," Asperilla responds while standing against the wall with a frown on her face.

"I know and that's why we are staying. This is our city."

Asperilla storms toward him. The ladies aren't sure to stop her or let the episode play out.

She paused inches away from his face. "I love you."

She grips his shirt and delivers an emotional kiss.

"Ahem," Ayanna interrupts. "Get a room."

Malakai checks his watch. "I must get ready, but you all sit back and prepare for the greatest show on Earth," he boasts.

He rushes to the secret elevator, presses the third floor, and rides to his office suite. Picture frames, spoken word albums, and mic stands are displayed the way he left them. "Damn it feels good to be back."

He runs to his favorite window and stares into the crowd. Two years ago, he would have masturbated watching a sexy woman grind her ass on the dance floor. He knows those days are over and happy being with Asperilla. She's the perfect mother and wife.

He spins away from the window and opens the door to his walk-in closet. He rolls his tongue and visualizes spitting poetry in the lycra shirt with tie, thigh shorts, hat, handcuffs, and badge. He undresses and transforms into a nasty cop. He adjusts the hat, walks to the mirror, and admire his poetic style. He tugs on his dick through the shorts. "Asperilla I promise I wouldn't pull my dick out, but they will see this gigantic print."

He shakes his dick a few times before skipping to the computer chair. He scrolls through his notes and rehearse.

He smiles devilishly once he finishes. "Yep! This is a pussy grabber."

He jumps from the seat, runs out the door, and down the hall to the elevator. He presses the button and heads to the rooftop.

Once the doors open, he walks to a secret opening displaying the stage perfectly. He knows this entrance will be like none other.

"Good Evening Malakai."

He turns and responds. "You must be the assistant. Is everything ready?"

"Yes, Sir! The zip line is set for your grand entrance."

Malakai slaps him on the back. "It would have been better if I made my return naked."

The assistant fastens the last hook. "Once you hit the stage, the floor crew will release you," He briefs.

"Wow! This is going to be one hell of a ride."

"Are you ready?"

"Fuck Yeah!"

He scans the crowd while he waits for his cue.

The pyrotechnic shoots from the stage and startle the crowd. The smoke clears, and the lighting tech shifts the beam toward the ceiling.

The bass line from *"Here I Go"* by *Mystikal* drops. Malakai dances as the crowd claps and cheers him on.

He pumps his fists, grips the bar, and plunge to the stage while screaming, "Da Poet Rite Chea."

The music plays as the crew secure and unfastens him. He thrust his pelvis and taunts the ladies in the front.

"Ya'll muthafukkas ain't ready," He screams and grips his dick.

He squats, flickers his tongue, and humps the ground. He rises and soaks in the applause. He slides his finger across his neck, instructing the sound engineer to kill the music.

He slings his hat in the crowd and rips his shirt; exposing his rip pecs and hard nipples. He stares over at Asperilla in the VIP section. Her eyes are shooting fiery darts. He knows not to drop anything else or she will fuck him up tonight.

"Love Divine, the poet right chea," he screams.

"Malakai, Malakai, Malakai," the crowd chants.

"Damn it feels good to be home," he thinks.

He silences the crowd once he blew his breath over the mic head. The room pauses and anticipates his first words.

"I want to taste you, is that alright? Tasting everything that makes you alive. If you were a cat, I'll suck out your nine lives plus your afterlife. Fold you like yesterday clothes and suck out your soul. Leaving your scent under my nose where my mustache used to be. When I step outside, the wind blows the scent of your memories."

"I'll eat you to sleep; swallow your heartbeat. I'll be so deep… that I'll know the time and the day of your period next week. I am a fucking Cunnilinguist. The way I eat, I should be a damn genius. Because E =mc2 means eating equal multiples orgasms whenever I place my mouth there.

"I'm in the mood to try all positions as my tongue make you tap to sexual submission. When was the last time someone ate you out until you blacked out?"

A Latino woman graces the stage in a mini skirt. Slides her thong over her heels and tosses them at Malakai.

He catches her thong in his mouth, pulls them out, and tucks them in his shorts.

He grabs her hand, drops to his knees, and restarts his piece as she rubs her hand over his head.

"I want to take it there tonight. Sucking on your breasts and fingering your holes. I'm the reason the ozone has a hole. I love making you wet. Ride my face like you are

*upset. Murder me. Drown me. Do whatever you want to me
because I want to see you happy."*

*"This is the best way to propose. Will you cum for me?
Tonight is all about you and this has been long overdue.
Washing your head like my tongue has been dip in
shampoo."*

*"Jump in and out of that pussy like my tongue is
connected to a bungee cord. Flickering your clit with my
fingers and licking you in between. Picking up the pace and
I love the way you taste. We have the perfect rhythm and
your climax is ready to explode."*

*"I feel you cumming down my face, leaving you with a
beautiful smile.*

"Ain't you glad I tasted you tonight?

"Ain't that alright."

He runs his fingers between her thighs and inserts them
into her mouth.

She slurps his fingers clean before he pulls them out.

He whispers on the mic. "How do you taste?"

He presses the mic to her mouth, and she moans,
"Delicious."

"I owe you, Joselyn. Thanks for assisting me."

"It's my pleasure. You can put on my thong and we'll
call it even. I can resell them like the dress and don't have
to worry about Nikki anymore."

He gives her a hug and escorts her backstage.

The crowd continuously cheers his name. He returns
and takes a bow.

"Thanks for coming out tonight. It's always an honor to
perform. I love you all."

"We love you too," the crowd yells.

"Please give me a moment and I'll be down shortly to
mingle."

He walks to the elevator and rides to his office. His adrenaline is pumping, and his mind is on the performance. He enters the office with a towel over his face.

Two guys catch him slipping and slings him against the wall.

Corbin spins around in his chair, "Awesome performance," he congratulates while clapping his hands. "I see why Necole was obsessed with you."

Chapter 21

Asperilla snaps her fingers to the music and grinds in her seat while watching the crowd.

"Are you going on the floor?" Jaz asks.

"I think I'm going to sit right here and wait on Malakai to come."

"Speaking of coming... Where is Ayanna?"

"Beats me," Cherry answers while shrugging her shoulders.

"She went to the restroom before Malakai's poem was finished," Asperilla says.

"They probably fucking," Jaz blurts.

Asperilla pulls out her blade and flips the switch. "I'll cut his balls off and slice her nipples."

"Girl put that meat cleaver away before you have us in jail again," Cherry jokes.

"How you get that shit in here anyway?" Jaz inquires.

"I stay strapped. Never know when war comes with your enemy," Asperilla responds.

Asperilla stands from the seat. "Anyway, I'm going upstairs to check on him."

She parts her way through the crowd and Jaz words replays in her head. *"They might be fucking!"*

She presses the elevator button and grins about the pussy she shared with Malakai. The elevator chimes and the doors slide open revealing a quiet but eerie hallway.

"Umm, if he's fucking it's not Ayanna because she's a screamer and creamer," she remembers.

"Somethings not right," she mumbles under her breath.

She lifts her skirt and slides her *Glock* from her body shape holster. She tosses her heels to the side, creeps to the door and listens to the sounds inside the room.

She notices manly voices, but something tells her the room is not friendly. "*1, 2,*" she counts slowly in her head.

She smashes the door with her foot and runs in with her Glock. "Let him go or die," she promises while pivoting her gun.

The men pull their guns and point them at her, "Put yours down."

Everyone is trigger happy from the commotion and unexpected surprises.

She yells, "No, muthafuckas put yours down."

Malakai walks over, kisses her cheek and slides his hand over her Glock. "It's ok baby, I got this."

"Who the fuck are they?"

Corbin spins from the window. "Asperilla I'm so excited that you can join the party."

He rises from the seat, smiles and pats Malakai on the shoulder. "You and Asperilla are Bonnie and Clyde reincarnated and perfect for each other."

"What's perfect is your dead ass next to your bitch," She guarantees.

Corbin chuckles to himself and responds, "Well if I came here strapped with a wire you would be in jail."

She shrugs her shoulders, "Been there… Done that. Corbin, why are you here?"

"Gentlemen, please put away your weapons. Go downstairs and enjoy the sexy atmosphere. Fuck some women and run the tab up."

The scene diffuses and Asperilla slaps the head of the last man walking out the door. "Get the fuck out."

She put her gun away and stares at Malakai. "Why the fuck you so quiet?"

"I'm waiting to hear what he has to say."

He stands eye to eye with Corbin, balls his fist, and turns up his nose. "You were smart… very smart to meet me at my club. You knew I would fuck you up elsewhere."

"You wouldn't do shit if we were outside the club," Corbin taunts.

Corbin glances in Asperilla's direction and tosses her a phone. "Here you go, pretty lady. A video call will be coming for you shortly."

She catches the phone and it buzz seconds later flashing Ayanna's face.

"Ayanna are you safe?"

"No, Corbin and his goons kidnapped me from the restroom. They are holding me hostage unless you do what he wants."

The wrinkles in her forehead appears as she reveals her sensitive side. "Ayanna, don't worry, we will take care of everything."

"Oh, I'm not worried but you should be," Ayanna cautions.

"What the fuck are you talking about?"

Ayanna flips the video screen and reveals a man holding a gun to Isabella's head.

"I told you I'm ok, but your family is not. Oh, it gets better, follow me."

She hovers the phone over Graciana's crib. "Here's the princess of the empire," she presents.

Asperilla bites her lips and exhales from her nose. "Bitch if you hurt my baby, I promise you won't live to regret it."

Ayanna brushes off the threats and displays a black bag on the phone. "Asperilla, I have a present for you."

"Get over here and hold this phone," Ayanna yells at Isabella.

She digs through the bag and pulls out an enormous anaconda. "I wonder how long it will take for the snake to swallow your precious baby."

Asperilla's voice becomes weak from the horrible visual. "Ayanna, don't do this, kill me instead," She pleads.

"I can't believe the baddest woman on the planet is submitting to her bottom bitch."

Malakai grabs the phone, "You are working for Corbin now, after everything we did for your ass."

Ayanna laughs and responds, "You two are a thorn in my ass. By the way Malakai, in the words of the great *Tupac* That's why I fucked yo bitch."

"Ayanna you don't have to do this. It won't end well for you."

"Yes it will?"

"Asperilla parades around with her baby when she made me abort mine. She promised we would take over your empire and leave you penniless. I bet she never told you that. You think Pandora was the only woman she was fucking. I was the main chick and she betrayed me once you became faithful. You should have stayed a whore and a poet," Ayanna confess.

Ayanna ends the video and the screen goes black.

Malakai and Asperilla bolts to the door.

"Sit your ass down," Corbin yells. "Your baby and Isabella will be fine. Have a seat."

Malakai turns around and says, "You are pushing my buttons."

Their eyes are saddened for the first time in their life. They sit down and prepare to listen.

Corbin rolls his sleeves up. "It's about to get deep in here for you two. Malakai, have you ever played chess?"

"Don't waste my time with board games."

Corbin ignores him. "Asperilla, have you ever played?" She doesn't respond.

"Spit it out!" Malakai yells.

"Hostile, are we? Now you see how it feels to lose something you love," Corbin acknowledges. "Listen, let's make this quick. You morons stole my better half and you will pay. I want her remains," he demands.

He opens a briefcase and pulls out two separate contracts. "Malakai, you will sign over your club, homes, and bank accounts. Asperilla your contract will include a one-way deportation back to Tijuana where your darkest enemies await. If you refuse then your baby dies, and my star witness will testify about the illegal sex trafficking. I'll make sure you two rot in hell until your last breath escapes your soul."

He slides the pen. "The decision is yours."

They stare at each other and ponder the decision. Without saying a word, they sign the contract.

"Excellent decision."

Corbin struts to the door and pause before stepping out. "Oh, before I forget, there's a way your baby can live."

"What's that?" Asperilla asks.

He smirks at Asperilla and responds, "You will love this idea. You have thirty days to deliver a head I can place on my mantle."

"Whose head? We have killed before and this should be easy," Asperilla confess.

"Great! I want your head or Malakai's head. It will sit perfectly next to Nikki's urn. I will enjoy watching you two kill each other."

He checks his watch. "Time flies, it's after 12. Now you have 29 days. Drinks on me tonight since this is my club now. Malakai, you should consider playing chess. Tonight, ya'll were served. Checkmate," He calls out and walks out the door.

Chapter 22

Malakai and Asperilla sit in silence and contemplate their next moves after receiving the news about Graciana abduction.

He touches Asperilla shoulder. "It's time to go home and check on Isabella."

She refuses to move and places her head on the table and cries.

"Asperilla, I'm sorry all of this is happening. We will get Corbin, but your cousin needs you right now."

"What about my baby? She needs-, never mind," she pauses and runs to the restr0oom. Her mascara smears her face as she daps her cheeks with a towel. *"Get a grip Asperilla, you have seen worse. You can defeat this."*

She puts on her tough girl persona and returns, "I'm ready."

He pulls her to his chest, grazes his fingers through her hair, and consoles her. "Don't worry, we will get her back."

She snorts her nose and tilts her head upwards. "I can't lose my baby."

He kisses her lips and squeezes her tighter. "You won't."

"You remember my favorite movie and how I wanted to remix it?"

"Yes, but I don't care about a damn movie right now. Our house is bugged, and they are probably watching us."

"Well on the way home think about it because it's the only plan I can think to save us."

They exit the club through the back to avoid everyone. They were almost there when they hear a voice. "Malakai! Malakai! Wait up!"

Monique runs swiftly and catches them. "Where are you going? There are people asking for your autographs. It's not like you to disappear after a performance. Is everything ok?"

"Yeah, we are fine but do me a favor."

"Sure."

"There's a crack on my first album. Please make sure it's restored to its original value."

Monique senses goes on full alert once he mentions the album. "I'm on it."

"Thank you and I'll call you later."

He leads Asperilla out the door and buckles her in the passenger seat.

"Where to Mr. Malakai?" The driver asks.

"Home and quick as possible."

The driver turns the corner and depart the club.

They didn't make eye contact throughout the ride. He glances out the window and counts the stars to clear his mind.

"How the hell I didn't sense Ayanna's betrayal" he ponders.

The driver arrives at the house in record-breaking time. "Thanks for getting us home safe and I'll see you on the next one."

"Do you need anything, Mr. Malakai?"

"Nah, I'll take it from here. Tell your family I said hello."

"I will."

He pulls an envelope from his pocket and hands it to the driver. "Go take the vacation you always talked about. I'll call you when I need you again."

"Thank you."

Malakai opens the door and carries Asperilla in the house. Isabella stands with her head down and afraid to face us. Her hands are trembling, and she steps aside without saying a word.

He carries Asperilla to the sofa and wipes her forehead.

Isabella leaves the door open and wishes she could run away.

"Isabella is suffering from shell shock and Asperilla is balled up on the couch. *"Damn, tonight won't be easy."*

"Isabella, it's alright. Come over here."

She eases over and sits a distance from them. She takes a deep sigh. "Malakai it wasn't my fault. Things happen so fast. I wa… wa… was."

"Slow down Isabella."

"Take it easy. I'll get you some tea, it will calm your nerves."

Minutes later she hears Asperilla whispering her name. She lifts her head and waves her over.

She hesitates but she didn't want to upset her. Isabella sits next to her but stares at the wall.

"Isabella, what happened to my baby?"

"Do you want to wait on Malakai to return from the kitchen before I explain?"

"Hell no. Fuck him. It's his fault too."

"Asperilla, I'm sorry I fucked up."

"Girl, I don't want to hear that shit. Just tell me what the hell happened."

"I put her to sleep and dozed off watching TV. A noise startled me, and I thought someone was in the house. I checked around, but it wasn't anything. I heard the noise again and my first instinct was to grab her and hide in the closet. We hid until I heard Ayanna call my name. I came out and met her in the hallway. She claimed you sent her to check on us. I went downstairs and things seem fine until an unknown man appeared from the kitchen with a gun aimed at me. I shielded behind Ayanna but all she did was laugh and snatched Graciana."

"Is that all?" Asperilla interrupts.

"Everything happened so fast. I don't remember all the details. I'm sorry and I wish I could have done more."

"You should have died protecting my baby!!"

"Huh, I'm not a killer like you Asperilla. I did what I could."

"Not enough."

Asperilla jumps from her seat, pulls her gun from her skirt, and points it at her. "Bitch, let's see what you can do with my gun pointing at you."

Isabella backpedals away. "No, Asperilla, don't do this."

"Don't do what?"

She squeezes the trigger and the round passes her head and pierces the wall.

Malakai runs out the kitchen. "What the fuck are you doing? Twice in one night you are drawing your gun on someone."

"Oh, you are taking this bitch's side. You are always putting another woman before your wife… maybe I should kill you too. You heard what Corbin said, A life for a life." I'll serve your fucking head on a platter and get my baby back."

He walks toward her attempting to disarm her. "You are upset and not thinking clearly. Don't allow him to corrupt our family."

She drops the gun to the floor and sits on the sofa. "You are right. I'm not sure what came over me."

He turns to check on Isabella. "Go pack your things, you are going home. Things are about to get ugly and we don't…"

"Malakai, watch out!" Isabella screams.

Asperilla leaps from the sofa and stabs him in the back with a knife hidden in her thigh garter.

His reaction causes him to backhand her in the face. She flips over the sofa and hit her head on the floor.

Isabella runs to him, "You are bleeding."

"Yeah, and it hurts like hell."

He grabs Asperilla's gun and advises Isabella to follow him to the vault. "Let's get out of here," he orders.

"The car is outside. I can drive you to the hospital."

"We won't make it out the yard."

"How dare you put your hands on me. You will die when I get my other gun," Asperilla vows and runs in the next room.

They sprint toward the unsecured vault. "*Damn, Ayanna memorized the code; that's how she got in the house.*"

"I'm coming for ya'll."

He pushes Isabella in the vault, "Get your ass in there." He closes it before Asperilla could reach them.

She snatches the outside phone and presses the number to dial inside. "You ain't shit."

"Asperilla, you are going too far."

"You put your hands on the wrong bitch."

"Asperilla it wasn't intentional, and you know I would never hit you."

"It doesn't matter since you are running away with my scary ass cousin and leaving me alone to get our daughter."

"You are losing it and need time to calm down."

"Nigga, they kidnapped my daughter and you are asking me to be calm. Fuck you and Isabella's bitch ass. You will die here, and I will get her back. Believe that!"

She hangs up the phone and walks away.

Isabella stares at him, "What are we going to do?"

"There's a secret tunnel we can escape through."

"Does Asperilla know where it leads?"

"Naw, I only told one other person. Let's go before she breaks in and find us."

They travel through the tunnel until they reach a dead end.

"Where to now?"

"Up," he responds pointing.

They climb the ladder and opens a latch to a door leading to an old garage.

He grabs the first aid kit off the workbench, "Help me apply this pressure dressing until I get some help."

"What about the knife?"

"Pull it out."

"Are you sure?"

"I will toughen you up before all of this is over. Now pull the damn knife!"

She wraps her hands around the handle and snatches it. He instructs her applying the field dressing as blood pours.

She completes the task. "I hope I did it right?" She asks.

"It will do. Hop in the car," He responds.

He flips the visor and the keys drop in his hands. He starts the ignition and drives pass his house laughing after seeing his house in flames.

Isabella is shocked. "You and my cousin are made for each other. Grace was kidnaped, Asperilla stabs you, burns down the house, and you are laughing."

"Yeah, I hate giving my enemy satisfaction or the last laugh. Let's go before the police comes."

"What about Asperilla? Is she in there?"

"Asperilla is probably heading to the airport to kill you."

"Why?"

"You left with her husband and let her daughter get taken."

"Where should I go?"

"Far away but you're not going home; it's too risky. I have friends coming to protect you until this is over."

"Malakai, please don't hurt her."

He drives out the neighborhood and assures, "I won't hurt her but there's no telling what she would do to me. Sit back and get some sleep. The sun will be rising soon, and we have a long day ahead."

She turns on the radio, leans back, and prays the music soothe the excruciating scenes from tonight's madness.

Chapter 23

Corbin leans against the rail of his yacht, sipping champagne, and gloating over his first chess move. He left them with a long sad expression on their faces.

He checks his watch and shakes his head. "Damn, what's taking Ayanna so long to arrive with the package?"

He paces back and forth over the deck until a car beep below. He races downstairs and asks, "Where is she?"

"Hmph! Good morning to you too Corbin," Ayanna retorts.

"Please forgive my manners. I am anxious to see the princess of Malakai's dynasty. You have no idea how it feels to have his seed in my hands," he exclaims.

She shoves the seat carrier in his chest. "Carry this, I'm tired of looking at her ugly ass. She reminds me of her funky ass mama."

He pulls the cover and reveals her beautiful brown eyes. "Aww, you are truly a diamond. I have no idea what Ayanna is talking about."

He takes them to the upper deck to meet the Spanish caregiver he hired earlier this week.

"Good Morning Ms. Garcia, this is Graciana. Make sure she has everything she needs."

She retrieves the carrier and responds, "Yes Sir, Mr. Lancaster."

He grabs Ayanna's hand and leads her through the doorway. "Follow me, we have plans to discuss."

She steps around him, goes straight to the liquor bar and pours a drink.

"It's a perfect day to celebrate," he brags.

"Fuck a celebration. I'm staying lit until Asperilla brings a hailstorm."

He pours a drink and sips confidentially. "Ahh…this champagne taste better the second time around. You don't have to worry about them. They will be trying to kill each other for the next thirty days."

"Thirty days Corbin? You are giving those idiots time to plot our deaths."

He smiles and massages her shoulders. "Baby, everything is going as planned. We will own their club, finances, and lives. I could have killed them, but death is too quick. They need to realize what it's like to lose it all."

She tilts her glass toward the playroom. "What about the baby?"

He chuckles and responds, "You can feed her to the anaconda once their tasks are completed."

She wraps her arms and kisses his lips. "Umm, sounds like a devious plan but you left out one minor detail."

"What's that?"

"My fucking promotion."

He winks his eye. "Ooh, I love when you get angry. Stay put, I got something you will like."

He walks to the counter and pulls out a red folder. "Everything is notarized and becomes official after this mission."

She snatches the folder from his hand. "Let me read this shit and make sure you are not pulling my leg."

She swiftly flips through the pages and scans the clause making her Tampa's top district attorney.

"Ayanna, you could be a district attorney anywhere. Why Tampa?"

"Tampa is home and I plan on running the biggest escort service in the state. Once you become governor all your contacts will be mine."

"We will own this state and soon the country," he indicates.

He slips his tongue into her mouth and savors the wine she drank earlier. He fondles her breasts and bites on her neck.

"Excuse me, Mr. Lancaster," security guard interrupts.

He doesn't acknowledge him and continues sucking on her earlobes.

She is in pure ecstasy and knows she will be getting dick soon. She moans and suddenly open her eyes.
"Oh shit!" she yells.

He feels her body trembling. "Yes baby, I'll have you vibrating in your secret spots."

She pushes him away and adjusts her clothes. "No fool, turn around," she notifies.

His voice freezes once he realized why the guard interrupted him.

Asperilla waves her hand. "Hola! Hate to be a cock blocker but we have unfinished business to discuss."

"What the fuck is she doing here?" Corbin asks.

"I caught her snooping around the yacht, and she demanded to see you," the guard responds.

Ayanna stands with her arms folded and interjects. "Bitch, you always fucking up a perfect moment."

"I knew you were the boss of the operation. I love a take charge, ask question later type of woman," he admits.

He motions to the guard. "Let her go and I'll call when I'm ready for you to appear with the package," he announces.

The guard pushes her forward causing her to stumble a few steps. She recovers her balance before falling. "Damn, you don't have to be so rough."

Asperilla uses her index finger and thumb to demonstrate a gun, and points at Ayanna.

Ayanna rolls her eyes. "Corbin, you better get her before I kill her ass."

"Calm down ladies, I'm sure we can handle this like civilized adults. Asperilla I thought I made myself clear on my terms."

He returns to the bar, refills his drink, and flushes it down.

"Asperilla would you like some?"

"No thanks; drinks and yachts aren't my cup of tea anymore."

Asperilla walks to the bar and pulls out a seat. "Okay Corbin, I need two guards, preferably not the ones I followed from my burning home to here."

"What makes you think I can trust you?" Corbin asks.

"You have my daughter and that's all the leverage you need. Plus, I'm the only one who can get under Malakai's skin. I know you watched me stab him and burn down our home last night."

"Yeah, I enjoyed every minute."

He gives her a business card. "Call this number and they will be at your disposable."

Ayanna huffs. "Corbin, I can't believe you are playing along with this manipulator. She can't be trusted."

He slides a glass down the bar. "Have a drink Ayanna, you are too tense. I will enjoy watching them spilling each other's blood."

"You heard him, have a drink. Better yet, go get my damn baby," Asperilla demands.

"I'll get her and feed her ass to the sharks," Ayanna responds.

"We both know he won't go for that. Be a good house pet and fetch."

"Asperilla, you can have your baby back once you deliver Malakai and Nikki's remains."

Ayanna and Ms. Garcia return with Graciana. "Here's your fucking gremlin," Ayanna says.

Asperilla lifts her daughter from Ms. Garcia arms. "I love you and everything will be okay," she whispers.

Asperilla speaks phrases in Spanish before Corbin rudely interrupts her. "Ahem, time for you to go. You have seen your daughter, she's safe and our deal is bounded with a head."

Asperilla returns the baby to Ms. Garcia. "You are right, thank you for your hospitality."

He presses an alert button and a guard appears minutes later. "Mrs. Valdez has overstayed her welcome. Please escort her off the yacht."

"Yes sir."

He heads back to Ayanna, "Your ex-boss is fearless and determined."

"Fuck her! I'm pissed she showed up. Promise me, no more interruptions because my pussy misses your mouth."

He presses the intercom, "Strengthen security and don't disturb me."

He lifts Ayanna in the air. "Let's go make war, fuck love," he quotes.

Chapter 24

Malakai drives to a secret cabin he purchased years ago to escape the city. Quietness, wild animal life and nature equals a day of calmness.

He turns off the car and shakes Isabella, "Wake up sleepy head; we are here."

She yawns, opens her eyes and stares at an old cottage. "Where are we?"

"Off the grid, for now."

He jumps out the car and opens her door, "People are waiting for us."

They march up the gravel pathway and knock on the wooden door.

"You sure they are here?" Isabella asks.

"They better be."

He knocks again and no response.

"Hands in the air and don't turn around," a female voice shouts from behind.

The door opens and two masked gunmen sits inside. "Get in here and don't do anything stupid," the second masked man commands as he tosses an envelope.

"Read it!" He says.

She rips it open. "*You are never safe. Corbin has eyes everywhere.*"

"Kill the bitch!" The male shouts.

She wasn't afraid to die this time and if this was her punishment for Graciana being kidnapped she wouldn't go down without a fight.

She wrestles the gun away fighting courageously and biting the gunman hand.

Isabella retrieves the gun and squeezes the trigger. Water squirts on the gunman mask.

"What the fuck is this!" She shouts.

She snatches off the mask, revealing a beautiful Asian woman. During the fight of her life, Isabella never noticed why Malakai wasn't fighting.

She throws the mask, "You knew all along. That's fuck up."

Malakai laughs and responds, "Yeah, I wanted to make sure you wouldn't sell me out when Asperilla comes. Let me introduce you to the family. On the floor is Mei and behind you is her sister Meiying."

Meiying snatches off her mask, "Nice to meet you Isabella."

He brings his attention to the center of the room, "And our third guest is none other than the infamous Kryptonite."

He pulls off the mask slowly and gives her a big hug. "Looks like we have a fighter on our hands."

Her breathing returns to normal and has proved to Malakai she's a survivor.

"Would you like something to drink?" Kryptonite asks.

"Yes, toss me some water. Mei wore me out, wrestling like a WWE Diva."

Mei erupts with laughter and flexes her biceps. "I'll beat all those bitches' asses."

Kryptonite interrupts, "Ladies, I wish we could stay but Malakai and I have some business to discuss. Please make sure Isabella has everything she needs."

Malakai turns his head back, "Meiying, I need your hands and thread later."

"I gotcha boo," she responds.

He shuts the door and runs to catch up with Kryptonite. They stroll through the woods and down to the lake.

"This place is relaxing Malakai. Inhale the peace; observe the tranquility. This is how life supposed to feel, not with drama surrounding your life."

Malakai slings a stone and watches it skips over the lake." I had peace; my life was perfect until Ayanna betrayed me."

He places his hand on Malakai's shoulder, "We all play the fool sometimes, but we are here to assist with taking your enemy down and getting your family back."

Malakai shakes his head, "Nah I'm not asking you to be involved with this nonsense between Corbin and Ayanna. I'll handle them."

"We are family; we take care of each other," Kryptonite reminds him of their bond.

"I know and I truly thank you but I'm only asking you to get my daughter and I'll handle the rest."

Kryptonite stares at the dry blood on Malakai's shirt. "Looks like you can't handle shit from where I'm standing."

Malakai tugs on his shirt and peeps over his shoulder. "Aww, it not that bad. It's not bleeding anymore."

"I told your ass to move overseas with me, but you wanted to get married and become a family man. My Mama always said a hard head makes a soft ass and you've been soft since Love Divine was killed. It wasn't your fault Malakai. You need to find balance, one minute you *Kill Bill* and the other minute you are friends with your enemy. Speaking of enemies, how are you going to deal with Asperilla?"

He throws another rock across the pond and turns around slowly, "I haven't figured that part out, maybe love will conquer all."

Kryptonite laughs in his face and responds, "Keep dreaming. She stabbed you in the back and probably will slice your neck next time. Corbin has been playing stupid ass mind games. Your daughter will end up with one parent or maybe none if you don't get your head right."

He gives Malakai a hug, "We will keep her safe until this blows off, I promise. Okay, that's my pep talk for today I'm heading back inside. Don't bring your ass in the house until you have a plan."

He watches Kryptonite disappear up the trail but having Corbin, Ayanna, and Asperilla is a deadly triple threat. He ponders if it came down to him and Asperilla, would he have the heart to kill her?"

He sits near the lake, reminiscing about the moment she changed his life by saving him from Necole's crazy ass.

He nods off. Lying motionless, he dreamt of being home holding Graciana on the back patio. Sun beaming, birds chirping, and the neighborhood is full of life. She falls asleep and he places her in the crib.

Asperilla calls his name as she relaxes in the hot tub, "Hurry up the water is relaxing."

He strips out his clothes, jumps in and suck on her lips. She pushes his head down, begging for him to eat her under the water. He descends, splitting her thighs, and plunging deep into her.

"Deeper," She moans.

She thrust her clit over his tongue, squeezes her thighs tighter around his head. He knows she is about to cum and holds his breath until she erupts then everything becomes calm. He taps the side of her thighs. She doesn't respond. He wrestles to break free, but she squeezes harder and holds his head.

His mind has willpower, but his body is lacking. He is unsuccessful as his body trembles and oxygen drops.

Asperilla laughs and shouts, "Die muthafucker, die."

He feels someone shake him as he gasps for air and opens his eyes.

"Malakai what the hell is wrong? You have been nonresponsive for the past five minutes," Isabella says.

He catches his breath, wipes his face, "Bad dream, I thought I was dying, and it wasn't shit I could do."

"Let's go in the house; you need to lie down," she mentions and grabs his hand.

He follows her and for the first time he is afraid of his demons.

Chapter 25

Meiying opens the bedroom door, "Zǎo shàng hǎo Malakai."

He sits up. "Good Morning Meiying. Where are my clothes?"

"I took them off."

His eyes scroll to his limp dick. He flips it and allows it to hang against his inner thigh. "Did we fuck?"

"No silly ass. You have a lovely specimen, but I didn't touch it. Remember the tea I gave you before I stitched your wound? It was laced with my family's secret to calm anxiety. You fell asleep and slept like a baby."

He cracks his neck, walks toward the mirror, and observe his back. "You did a wonderful job."

He kisses her cheek.

She smiles and points toward his dick pressing on her thigh.

"Oh, Shit Meiying, I forgot about my third leg."

"What a waste of good dick; you could have made a fortune in my city. Put some clothes on and meet us in the den," she says and closes the door.

He enters the bathroom, takes a refreshing shower, and replays every conversation between him and Ayanna concerning Corbin.

"There must be a weak link in their plans."

He finishes his shower, finds a jogging suit and joins the family in the den.

Sniffs his nose in the air, "Umm, something smells good."

He strolls in and sees Isabella cooking. "Slow down, you are beating the hell out of them," he says.

"No Papi, I drum my eggs. The taste is in the rhythm."

"What did you say?"

"Taste is in the rhythm."

"No, before that."

"I drum my eggs."

He slaps his hand against his thigh. "That's it Drummond! Ms. Drummond is the name Ayanna mentioned. Yo, Kryptonite, check this shit out."

He rushes to the table, "There is a woman working for Corbin named Ms. Drummond. I'm sure she is pissed with Ayanna being on board."

"What makes you sure?"

"Ayanna told me a few times how nosy she is and always in the way. We find her. We find my daughter."

"You know anything about her?" Kryptonite asks.

"Not exactly but I know who will."

He walks to the closet and finds the secret phone. Dial a special code and wait for it to ring. "Undercover Brothers, may we help you?"

"Good Morning, this is Malakai. I know it has been a long time, but I need a background check on a woman."

"What's her name?"

"She's an Associate DA for Corbin Lancaster."

"Okay, that will be our normal fee."

"I'll include a bonus if you can get it within an hour."

"Consider it done. I will call you back shortly."

He hangs up the phone and dials another special code to sync a three-way conference between Cherry and Jaz.

"This is Malakai, I need you all to meet me at the hanger."

"Is there anything we should know?" Cherry asks.

"Yeah, stay the fuck away from Asperilla & Ayanna. I'll explain when I get there. For now, gather your necessity and move quickly. Jaz, this is serious. Don't get caught slipping."

"Okay, I gotcha. I'll have my ass there and on time," Jaz responds.

"Alright, see ya'll later this evening."

They disconnect the calls and return to the family.

"What you need from us?" Mei asks.

"For you and Mei to recon the hanger and make sure there are no surprises."

His stomach growls, "I'm hungry as hell. Isabella, bring those pancakes and eggs to the table."

"Hold your mule, it's almost done," she yells.

Mei and Meiying assist her in the kitchen while Malakai sets the table.

"Kryptonite, are you going to do anything?" Malakai asks.

He shuffles the newspaper, "Nope, but I will eat when the table is set. I'm saving my energy; I'm not getting any younger."

The ladies bring the food with steam rising from the bowls and plates.

They take a seat, join hands and Malakai prays, "Heavenly Father, thanks for another day even when we're not worthy. Your protection is upon our soul. Thanks for blessing the union and providing this incredible meal for us. Keep us safe from our enemies. Please keep my wife and child under your grace. Asking for all these blessings in your son name... Amen."

After the food was eaten, Isabella stands and announces, "Fellas you do the dishes."

Malakai nods at Kryptonite, "I'm not sure about him but I'll clean up."

He completed the chore in thirty-five minutes. His secret phone rings before he could sit down and relax. "What did you find out?"

He gets the info and flashes a vengeance grin, "Thank you."

He hangs up and dances his way to the family.

"What the hell are you happy for?" Kryptonite asks.

His phone buzzes with a bio and a pic of Susan Drummond. He reads and scans everything before showing the picture to Kryptonite.

"Please take a moment to meet Ms. Drummond, Assistance District Attorney to Corbin Lancaster."

"She's a sexy vanilla bean with long legs," Kryptonite boasts.

"Glad you noticed because you are going to infiltrate his organization through her pinkness. She unwinds every Friday night at a secluded jazz spot. Kryptonite, you will love this part. She enjoys rough sex if she's attracted to you. Mei and Meiying, follow Ayanna and see what she's up to."

"We can't wait to get some action. We haven't done shit in Tampa since we castrated the pastor," Mei discloses.

Meiying swings her hands in the air, dances, and chants, "We're getting another trophy! We're getting another trophy!"

Malakai shakes his head, "Nothing has changed but have fun."

"Isabella?"

"Yes Malakai."

"While we are out, Kryptonite will teach you how to shoot. It's time for you to earn your stripes."

"Your plans sound good but what about the elephant in the room?" Kryptonite addresses.

All the eyes trail to Malakai. He clutches the bulge in his pants, "No worries, I'll keep my wife occupied."

Chapter 26

Mei and Meiying recon the hanger and position themselves behind the car.

Mei flips the safety switch on and off, "Damn, I was hoping I had a chance to unload a few rounds in a warm body by now."

"I know what you mean, this place is boring as fuck," Meiying responds.

Mei checks her watch and turns to Meiying, "I thought they were supposed to be here around eight-thirty. I'm calling Malakai to see what's going on."

She dials the number, "His phone is going to voicemail."

"I'm sure he has a reason. Go tell the pilot to start the plane," Meiying suggests.

Mei proceeds up the stairs, stops at the entrance, looks back, and smiles. "We might get some action after all. Behind you!" She shouts while pointing at the road leading to the field.

Headlights from a car appears from the darkness and travels at a high speed. Meiying eases her finger around the trigger and maintains her position.

The driver of the SUV turns the lights off and opens the back door slowly. Mei and Meiying remain in suspense.

Mei shines her flashlight on the SUV. The door swings with Jaz, Cherry, and her fiancé sprinting to the plane.

Meiying grabs Cherry, "Where the hell is Malakai?"

"He's coming. He said to get in position." Cherry states.

"Cut her loose and get your ass ready pilot for takeoff," Mei orders.

Mei drives the car and parks it against the SUV to create a barricade for the upcoming situation. She pops the trunk and grabs the M249 bag with her sniper rifle.

The airplane door closes, and propellers blow a strong wind. The lights flash and taxis down the runway.

Meiying watches as the wheel retracts and the plane disappears in the clouds.

"Holy shit!" Mei shouts.

A black *Crown Victoria* accelerating with a red Charger in pursuit approaches the airfield. The Charger fishtails the rear tire of the Victoria, causing it to spin out of control and crashes into a wall. The Charger decelerates and comes to a complete stop. The driver's door opens and Malakai steps out. "Mei, Meiying, is everyone safe?"

Mei comes out first, "Yeah, we are safe, but it seems you are the one with all the action. Who's in the car?"

"Some of Corbin's associates. They were watching Jaz's house. I followed and distracted them along the way to give everyone a chance to board the plane."

"What are we going to do with them?" Mei asks.

Malakai hunches his shoulders, "Do as you wish. Make sure you send a message to Ayanna and Corbin."

Mei flashes a sinister smile and runs to the driver door.

The airbags deployed and the men are bleeding and groaning.

Meiying sees her excitement and wants in on the action, "Hold up bitch, I'm getting some too."

They place their guns to the associates head. "Who do you work for?" Mei asks.

"Seriously Mei, you already know the answer. Let's teach them a lesson," Meiying says.

"I know but I was hoping they will say something smart, so I can feel violated," she jokes.

They smile at each other, squeeze the triggers, and screams, "Twin Power Activate," while firing a single shot simultaneously in each one of their heads.

Malakai stands and watches, "Wow, I thought you would have released more."

"Oh, we aren't done yet," Meiying responds.

Mei runs and grabs two *ARX-160* from the black bag and gives one to her sister. They stand on each side of the car, laugh while the bullets rip and jerk through their flesh.

Mei and Meiying place their guns down and hug each other. "Hell, yeah you saw that shit?"

Malakai claps his hands, "Thanks for the early Fourth of July; now get rid of your mess."

"We love cleaning as much as killing," Mei responds.

"We will meet tomorrow at the spot. Don't stay here all night," Malakai says.

He drives away from the airfield and activates his Bluetooth to call Kryptonite.

"Hello."

"The plane is in the air and I'll be back tomorrow."

"Why aren't you coming tonight? Never mind, I already know where you are going. I hope you have a large insurance policy messing with Asperilla."

"What can I say? You know how much I love her plus I need to make sure she's okay?"

"It's your death wish. I'll finish my plans for Ms. Drummond because people have work to do unlike you."

He disconnects the call and Malakai continues driving toward *Clearwater*. After 45 minutes, he arrives at the *Opal Sands Resorts*. He throws the keys to the valet and enters the lobby. The cool breeze from the *Gulf of Mexico* hits him as soon as he steps on the rose petaled lawn. He quickly reminiscences about their wedding.

His phone rings and quickly answers, "This is Malakai."

"I know who the hell this is. Bring your ass up here."

A dark shadow appears and waves him forward. He walks with caution, ensuring he isn't being set up. He takes the final steps under the arch and speechless once he stares into his wife's eyes.

"Relax, I'm not in the mood for blood tonight."

She nods her head toward the pillows and blanket.

"What's this for?" He asks.

"This might be the last time one of us watches a sunrise, so I decided to do it together."

"Asperilla, I have a pla—"

She places her finger over his mouth, "Hush, please enjoy this peaceful moment."

He kisses her with everything in his soul. If he dies tomorrow, she will remember this night.

He lies on his back and she rests her head on his chest. Neither spoke to each other.

A million things go through his head. He replays the dream of drowning during one of their spontaneous escapades. He ponders if Ayanna will come and put a bullet in his head. He shakes the thoughts away, runs his fingers through Asperilla hair and massages her back. It wasn't long before she falls asleep in his arms. He stays up and thinks of his daughter until the sun appears.

He hugs her tighter and kisses her lips, "Wake up baby, the sun is shining."

She yawns and mumbles in a groggy voice, "Thank you."

He wishes this moment could last forever but time is up. He uncoils himself and stands upright. "Thanks for the sunrise. Hopefully, I'll see you on the other side."

"Maybe but do me a favor?"

"What's that?"

"Don't let our love clutter your will to live. I will kill you without hesitation."

She spills her words without blinking, goes in a yoga pose and calmly meditates.

He turns around without looking back, exits the hotel, and drives back to the cabin.

Chapter 27

Ayanna rolls on Corbin, slides his dick into her wringing-wet pussy and rocks her hips.

"Umm, I love the way you wake me in the morning," he moans.

She rolls her tongue around his lips and plunge deep down his throat.

He breaks their kiss, bites her nipples and grips his nails in her ass cheeks.

He releases and whispers, "Ayanna."

"Yes baby."

"Do that thing."

"What thing?"

"You know what I mean, stop teasing me."

She smiles and spins on his dick in reverse. She does a Chinese split, lies her torso flat on the bed, and buries her face in the pillow.

He palms her ass with both hands and ram his dick. Her pussy gets wetter with every stroke.

"Harder Corbin beat this pussy. You know you love black meat; eat me!"

She drops her ass on his face, wiggle her left cheek, pause, and wiggle the right. She twerks as he parts them and licks her ass. Her body trembles from the sensational rush from his tongue. She jumps and smothers her juices over his nose. She looks over her shoulder and asks, "Are you ready for dessert daddy?"

He flickers his tongue on her clit as she recoils and twirls her hips. He sucks her moisture and inserts one finger into her ass while eating her pussy.

"Oh Shit! You never did that before."

She bucks her ass one last time before tickling her tongue over his dick. She opens her mouth and gobbles. She twerks and slurps causing Corbin to eat faster and harder. She anticipates his sweet cum running down her throat.

He continues eating and she loves it. He refuses to stop until she says it's time. She sucks vigorously; deep throating and spitting on it. She massages the head with her slimy saliva and watches it drool down the base. She dives down until her nose rests on his balls. She pauses at the base of his shaft and he thrusts his deeper into her throat.

He slides from under her pussy and speaks her magic words. "Yes baby, almost. Hold that mouth right there," he instructs.

He plants his face back in position, biting on her clit, and probing her with more fingers.

She erupts again over his face. Her juices run down his neck and over the sheets. He jabs her throat with ruthless aggression until he cums in her mouth.

He shivers and falls to the bed.

She devours his seed and sucks the leftover aftertaste from his mushroom head. She rises from the bed and wipes her mouth. "Damn, that was delicious. I'll jump in the shower."

He stares at the ceiling and waves his hand in the air. "Do whatever you like. I'm laying a little while longer."

Within 30 minutes, she returns and finds him sleeping like a baby.

She smiles and thinks, "*My pussy has always been the death blow for these men.*"

She slips on her robe, shoes and goes downstairs. She floats in the kitchen then freezes at the entrance; startled by Ms. Drummond sitting on the bar stool.

She turns her lips, "Don't you have paperwork to file, sign, or shred?"

Ms. Drummond sips her tea and places it on the table, "Ayanna, don't worry, I'm not here to interrupt your scandalous sex feast."

She reaches into her briefcase and retrieves some documents, "I'm here to make sure Corbin signs the final paperwork on Malakai and Asperilla."

"Whatever bitch! Hurry up and go," Ayanna yells.

"I'll go but don't get too comfortable. You are not his first love," she reminds Ayanna.

Ms. Drummond finishes her tea, hops off the chair and leaves. She stops and throws her index finger in the air and says, "Before I forget there's a package in the den for you lovebirds. I would have left it, but it was stamped with urgency all over it. Please make sure he receives it since you want my job so badly."

Ayanna peels her robe and reveal her mocha coke bottle figure. She slips a finger into her pussy, slides it out, and suck on it. "Umm, you wanna taste. This sweet pussy is the reason you are close to being terminated."

Ms. Drummond rolls her eyes in disgust. "Some ladies know how to keep things behind closed doors. Besides, Corbin will never fire me. I'm too valuable unlike your throwaway vagina," she acknowledges.

Ayanna charges toward her. "I have had enough of your smart-ass mouth. Bitch, I will whoop your ass!"

She grabs a handful of Ms. Drummond's hair and slams her to the ground.

"Help! Corbin help!" Ms. Drummond screams.

Minutes later Corbin rushes into the kitchen and lifts Ayanna off her. "Enough! Cut this shit out. We aren't the enemy. Why are you here so early anyway?"

"I came to drop off some documents and a package."

"What package?"

"The one in the den."

Corbin is followed by Ayanna and Ms. Drummond to the den. He sees a box written with the words "URGENCY" all over it. *"Must be Christmas,"* he thinks.

He rips the box and lifts two 32 oz jars of pickles and pickled eggs. "What the fuck is this back woods, down south shit?"

He sets them on the table, and discovers a sealed envelope addressed to him.

He gives it to Ms. Drummond. "Open it since you brought this craziness in my home", he says.

Her face is puzzled and very hesitant to open it.

"Open that shit, Susan!" He yells.

She jumps from his tone and rips the envelope as Ayanna snickers.

She pulls out a letter and reads, *"Dear Corbin, I'm honored to be a part of this chess game. You struck first by kidnapping my daughter and enticed my family to betray me. I'm not a chess player but I do make moves. I hope you would like some popular delicacies. Mmm, pickles and pickled eggs. You should try some and feed them to your bitches as well. Love, Malakai."*

He snatches the letter from her hand. "Give me this bullshit," he demands.

He rereads, tosses it down, and stares at Ayanna. "I've never seen a man who knows he's outnumbered and still like to play games. Malakai is alright with me, pass me one of those pickled eggs. I'll play his games, for now."

Ayanna passes him the jar and says, "I'm from Atlanta and my grandma used to can that shit. You can eat all you want but I'm not kissing you again."

"Why not? You already tasted my pussy," Ms. Drummond blurts.

"Oh, the uppity bitch has a foul mouth after all," Ayanna claps back.

Corbin stirs his hands in the jar while listening to them argue, "Stop all of that bickering; it is more than enough of me to go around."

He continues to stir, clamp his fingers down, pull an egg out, and opens his mouth. His cockiness distracts him from looking at what he is about to eat.

"Mr. Lancaster! Don't eat the-," Ms. Drummond screams.

Ayanna runs over and slaps it out of his hand.

"What the hell Ayanna?"

She places her hands over her mouth and points toward the ground.

He looks down, rushes to the kitchen and vomits in the trash.

"That nasty mutha- "He pukes again before finishing his sentence. He runs to the kitchen sink to rinse his mouth.

Ayanna hands him a towel. "Corbin, are you okay?"

"Fuck no! I almost ate a human testicle."

Ms. Drummond waltz in with the pickle jar. "There are two white penises floating around."

Corbin's face turns red with anger. "Get the housekeeper now; he will pay for this bullshit."

Chapter 28

Kryptonite sips his drink and listens to the music of *Akua Naru* and her live band.

He sits smoothly dressed in a creme *Sebastian Latte Lino Tweed Jacket* and *True Religion Jeans*.

He admires Ms. Drummond from a distance. She is wearing a two-piece strap short dress displaying her beautiful legs.

He scrolls through his phone and takes a double look at the picture Malakai sent. *"This photo serves no justice."* he thinks.

A waitress flirtatiously struts over, "Excuse me Sir, would you like something else to drink?"

"Not at this moment but before you go, please put whatever she's drinking on my tab," he says while pointing at Ms. Drummond.

The waitress' eyes open wide from the crisp bills he hands her. "I'll make sure to deliver it," she replies.

He scans the room and mumbles, "Tampa has some bad bitches. I can't believe Malakai left all this pussy on the table. I'll clean up after him like always."

He notices the waitress assuring Ms. Drummond of her courteous drinks.

She spins around in her chair and smiles. Her eyes quickly freefall between his legs.

He opens them wider and to give a glimpse of his dick print.

She tilts her glass in the air and turns back in her seat.

"Gotcha," he mumbles to himself.

He pulls out his cell and sends a text to his favorite ladies and within five minutes, Mei and Meiying greets him at the booth.

"What's the wager tonight?" Mei asks.

"Ten Grand, I'll be balls deep in her before the clock strikes twelve," he brags.

Meiying erupts with laughter and responds, "Speaking of balls, I'm sure Corbin loved our present."

He orders a round of shots, enjoys the music, but never takes his eyes off Ms. Drummond. He drinks and converses for thirty more minutes until he feels comfortable to make his move.

He checks his watch, "Ladies, it's showtime; deposit my money by tomorrow."

He glides from the table and eases over, "Good evening, were your drinks soothing?"

She is hesitant to respond but spills everything brewing inside of her. "Are there any decent men left on this planet because you all are full of shit? I come here to get away from my fucked-up reality and your sexy smile ruined my night."

He has been around many women and knows when a man has gotten under their skin.

She takes a deep breath and sips on her drink. She was ready to begin her rampage again but notices Mei and Meiying grabbing their things.

They make an unannounced stop at the bar, "Thanks for inviting me and my sister. We had a wonderful time. See you at work Monday," Mei says.

"Anytime ladies; make sure to let me know you all made it home."

"Sure thing," Mei responds and winks.

He watches them walk out the door and focuses his attention back on Ms. Drummond. Her mouth drops low from assuming he was like the previous guys she dated.

She throws her finger to signal the bartender, "Please double my next one I need it." She turns to face Kryptonite, "Please excuse my rudeness; it has been a long week. Can we start over?"

He slides his fingers through hers and tickles her palms as he pulls away, "Yes we can. My name is Kevin."

A sexual sensation rushes through her soul. Her body shivers from his slight touch.

"Are you ok?" He asks.

She gulps her drink and mumbles, "Mmm-hmm."

"Excuse me, I didn't catch your name."

She thinks to herself, *"Because my vagina was screaming it for me."*

"My name is Susan."

"Desperately Seeking?"

"I beg your pardon.

"No, Susan like the movie; the one with *Madonna*."

"Wow, you went way back."

He smiles from her comment.

Her mind wanders from being blinded by his pearly whites and thick tongue. *"Damn, there goes a charming smile again. I would love to have his mouth over me. Cut it out Susan, where is your self-control."*

She quickly switches the conversation. "Is this your first time here because I've never seen you before?"

"Yes, I love this band; the way they play the strings, blows the horn and beats the drums."

She watches his mouth move in slow motion as her pussy pulsates to the syllables he pronounces.

"Bartender! Please cash out my tab," he yells.

She rambles through her purse, "I can leave the tip if you like."

"No, you are fine. I will take care of it."

"You are such a gentleman, I'm glad I didn't leave.

"Likewise, now we can leave together."

"What makes you think I'm-?"

He leans in, yanks her hair, races his tongue up her neck and sucks her earlobes.

She didn't wear any panties tonight and he notices a single line of wetness run down her thighs. "I'm so embarrassed," she mumbles.

"No need."

He leans, slurps and responds, "Let's get out of here."

They exit holding hands and laughing.

"I love this city; beautiful nightlife, spontaneous events, and now a King in shiny armor saving me."

"Susan, where did you park?"

She's a little tipsy but alert. She fumbles through her purse, finds her keys and press the panic button.

"You are over here, nice ride."

"Thank you. I can't wait to test drive your stick."

He grabs her hand and places it on his dick, "Don't cash a check your mouth can't swallow."

"Ummm, I love when a man talks shit."

"You sure you not too tipsy for a nightcap. I can make sure you get home safely, and we can reschedule."

"Fuck that! I need some real dick in my life."

"Malakai was right, this bitch is a rough rider. I shall beat this pussy," he thinks.

She creates a scene and luckily most of the people are minding their business.

He hovers his hand over her mouth to keep her quiet and walk swiftly to her car. He escorts her to the passenger seat and runs around.

"Where to?"

"Kevin, you are too silly; it has voice commands."

He presses the talk switch and the navigation laminates.

"Go home!" She shouts.

The directions display, and he flashes a car before driving out the lot.

"Take your time driving. I'll take a nap to be fully energized for you."

She closes her eyes and within minutes, she dozes off.

He cruises down the street and looks over at her, "Sleep well, you will have a long night."

Chapter 29

He pulls in the driveway of her Westchase suburbia neighborhood. He admires her colorful condo and breathe in the serenade of the lake.

He walks around and gently shake her shoulders. "Susan, we have arrived."

She yawns and rolls out the car, "Thank you baby."

He gives her the keys and assists her to the front door.

She steps in and presses the numbers to deactivate her alarm. The hallway lights are motion sensored and illuminate our path to the spacious living room/ dining combo with the new whitewash wood floors.

She takes a sit on the stairwell. "Kevin, can you give me a hand?"

He stoops and slips off her heels like Cinderella.

"I'm going upstairs to find something more comfortable. Please make yourself at home."

He removes his blazer, drapes it over the sofa and flips on the TV to watch NBA highlights. He had been watching the show for about 30 minutes and realize no water was running upstairs. *"I hope this bitch hasn't fallen in the shower."*

He creeps upstairs and discovers her naked body, eyes closed with a Master Cock dildo.

"You love how creamy my pussy gets for you. I bet your cock is getting hard right now. You love how I turn you on. You like this tight, wet pussy. You know you wanna fuck me."

He continues to watch as she pinches her pink nipples and stirs the tip around her clit.

She slaps it over her swollen wet lips. "Oh, I can't wait until you fuck me."

She inserts deeper with only the balls in view. She bites her bottom lip and runs her hand through her hair. "Oh yeah."

She throws her legs in the air. "You make my pussy feels so good. Oh baby, I need you," she cries out.

She fucks herself faster, "Fuck yeah, baby. I feel all of that fucking cream dripping down my ass."

"Faster."

"Fuck me!"

"I will cum all over that hard dick."

"You going to make me cum."

"I'm so fucking close. Ooh, Ooh."

Her pussy speaks another language as he grips his dick and slowly undresses.

She speeds up the penetration and yells. "Aww, I'm cumming, I'm cumming."

She creams, pulls it out, and slurp the leftovers. She waves him over, "Come and beat this wet pussy," she orders.

He holds and shakes his veiny, thick, dark dick while walking, "Bitch, I won't be merciful."

She smiles and moans, "I don't care, just fuck me."

He snatches her off the bed and forces her to the ground. "Open your mouth bitch, spit on it!!"

He thrusts his dick down her throat causing her to gag. He grabs her head and rams her mouth harder and harder. She slurps and twists his dick.

He snatches his dick out, grips her throat, and slangs her on the bed.

"On your knees," he demands.

"You a nasty undercover slut. You getting this dick tonight," he assures her and slaps her ass.

He glides into her wet pussy and shoves two fingers in her mouth. "Suck your juices."

He yanks his fingers out and inserts them into her asshole to spread it wider. He slides his dick in and out her pussy while finger fucking her asshole.

She moans, "What are you doing?"

"Saturating that asshole. Don't worry I'll plug you once and for all."

He fucks her with harder strokes, "Arch that back bitch. Arch it," he demands again.

He slides out of her pussy and penetrates her asshole.

She gasps for a moment but takes all his inches.

He yanks her hair, pulling her back as he fucks her with powerful strokes. Gripping his nails in her ass cheeks and scratching her skin until red marks appear.

She loves it and screams, "Fuck me Kevin."

"You ready to ride this dick. "Tell me you ready."

She looks back. "Fuck that ass baby, fuck it good."

She hovers over him, slides his dick into her asshole, and bounce while waving her fingers over her pussy lips.

He clutches her obliques, forcing her while thrusting harder inside.

"Oh my God, yes," she wails.

She rides faster, and their rhythm is flawless. Her asshole clinches his dick as she ascends and descends over and over.

"My asshole hurts but don't stop."

He ignores her and bends her legs behind her head. He pulls his dick out for a split second and gazes at the crater that was once her asshole. It has swollen to the size of a golf ball.

"I want that cum in my ass. I fucking want it," she yells.

He breathes harder, "Almost."

He pumps faster and faster.

She moans harder.

"I'm going to spray in your ass, hold still, I'm cumming."

He pulls out, strokes his dick harder, and shoots cum like free throws inside of her asshole.

"Ahh, Ahh, it feels so warm," she confirms.

He spins around and walks to the bathroom. He washes himself and returns with a warm towel to clean her.

"Please open your legs."

She spreads as he takes his time between her thighs, and over her lips.

She moans, "Umm, I could taste you all night. No man has ever fucked me by force. I loved it."

He smiles, slips on his underwear, and walks to the door.

Her eyes lock in on his ass. "Damn, you are too fine; come back."

"I'm going to make some coffee. Tonight is going to be a long one for you," he assures.

He closes the door and she stares at the ceiling reflecting on the sex they created. Tonight, was her first time getting some dick since Corbin threw her away for Ayanna. She plays with her pussy and thinks of more kinky shit to do once he returns. She jumps from the bed, runs to her secret drawer and pulls out more toys.

She throws straps, handcuffs, blindfolds, and floggers over her head. She isn't looking where it lands. Once she feels satisfied, she jumps on the bed and waits for him.

There's a knock on the door.

"Come in."

Malakai walks in carrying a tray, "Sugar or cream?"

She quickly covers her exposed souls. "Where the hell is Kevin?"

"He's downstairs making a sandwich."

"Are you going to kill me?

"Susan, relax. You will live to see many tomorrows."

He sets the tray on the bed. She is hesitant so he takes a sip and passes her the cup.

She takes a sip, exhale, and blurts. "I had nothing to do with your daughter."

"I believe you but listen Corbin made us sign some papers and I need you to reword them."

She sinks deeper under the cover, only revealing her eyes. "What if I get caught?" She mumbles.

"You already getting fucked over by Corbin, and I can smell desertion pussy a mile away. I know you haven't been touched since Ayanna joined the organization," he admits.

"So, you're not going to kill me."

"No."

"What makes you think I wouldn't tell Corbin?"

He smirks and points toward the ceiling. "I hid a camera in your room when you were at the bar. I'll post your humiliating sex video on social media. Afterwards, I'll make sure they find a piece of you in 50 states if you fuck me over," he pressurizes. "Now, if you decide to work with me, I'll see to it that you are next in line for district attorney. I'm sure that's what you want anyway."

He rises from the bed and places the cup on the platter. "I'll send Krypto—I mean Kevin."

He chuckles out the room and jokes, "Once you taste black dick; it's hard to swallow other shit."

Chapter 30

Corbin returns from his trial delighted about the prosecution of another innocent man for a prison quota.

He has been making money on the side from private prison industries for years.

"America will never be great but it's a great place to live if you have power and wealth," he thinks.

He catches the elevator to the top floor of his penthouse office suite to meet his staff. He loosens his tie as he walks and slams the briefcase on the desk. "Today is a great day to fuck with Malakai. Where are we with Phase Two?"

Ms. Drummond gathers her notes and stands, "Mr. Lancaster, I believe taking over his club is the next agenda," she reports.

He smiles and rubs his chin. "Yes, I'll have my social gathering at his club and invite nothing but the elite."

He opens his briefcase and passes out some confidential documents. "My battle with Malakai has gone deeper than revenge. There's a rich bid on his head from some of my closest business associates. They want him alive to torture him in one of their private prisons. He not only ruined my life with Nikki, but he has fucked all their wives causing divorces, embarrassments and chaos in this city for over 10 years."

"Excuse me," Ayanna interrupts. "What if Asperilla kills Malakai?"

"I'm glad you asked," Corbin responds.

"Asperilla is a scorned Mother but won't kill him until her baby is safe. She's phase three of my plans and I have to make sure she brings Malakai to me."

"Afterwards, I'll slaughter their child, bury Asperilla alive, and send Malakai to prison forever. This meeting is adjourned except for Ms. Drummond."

The team exit the room and she feels appreciated being alone with Corbin. She bats her eyelashes as she approaches him. "I'm truly flattered you consider me special after all this time. I thought you hated me since Ayanna came and I'm glad you are giving me another chance. I won't let you down again. I have some good news as well. Guess who I met the other night?"

"Susan, before you get ahead of yourself. You're not my date for tonight and there's nothing wrong with me and Ayanna. I didn't want to single you out in front of everyone. You are here because you are going to compile the guest list and plan a party."

"So, you screw me for the past year and a half and now I'm trash? Fuck you, Corbin!"

"Watch your damn tongue when you are speaking to me. Don't act like screwing me wasn't beneficial. You would have been a public defendant forever if I didn't recommend you as an asset to my staff. Now as my Assistant DA, do as I request, or you will never work in this city again."

She stomps her feet and places her hands on her hips. "Your obsessions with Malakai have corrupted you or maybe it's Ayanna sucking the intelligence out."

He smiles and rubs his hands over his dick. "You didn't have a problem sucking me. You want one last taste?"

She slaps his face. "Kiss my ass!"

He laughs and responds, "Ayanna was right, you do have some hood in your white soul. This discussion is over."

"Have my party planned or don't bother showing up for work tomorrow. Now tell me what happened the other night?"

She rolls her eyes and proclaims, "Absolutely nothing."

"Okay, don't say I didn't ask."

He brushes besides her and walks out the door.

She sits in her chair, cries, and reminisced when Corbin used to make her feel like the next Mrs. Lancaster. She wipes her eyes. "Fuck him and Ayanna. I'll make sure they pay for this shit. Yeah, I sucked your dick, swallowed cum, and this is the thanks I get?"

She takes her frustration by tossing papers and flipping over chairs. She regathers the documents and Malakai's words pop inside her head. *"You could be the next DA."*

"My pussy nor throat will not be in vain because of his new whore. I have worked too hard to return to Andy's Trailer Park."

She rushes to the car with the documents and calls Malakai. By her surprise he answers on the first ring.

"Ms. Drummond, you have considered my offer?"

"What makes you think I didn't tell him?"

He chuckles, "Because your pussy begs for revenge. You wouldn't do anything like that. If I know your boss, I'm sure he pissed you off again."

She laughs and admits, "You are right. Fuck him! I wish he swallowed those balls inside the jar."

"Me too but you contacted me. How can we help each other?"

"This need to be discussed in public. When can you meet me?"

"Tonight is perfect."

"Will Kevin be there?"

"I'm not sure but I will ask him."

She blushes for a second and says, "Thank you."

"I will send you an address to meet me at 9 pm. Matter of fact, I will send Kevin instead," he suggests.

"Okay, I will be on time."

"Indeed, you will."

He disconnects the calls and yells, "Yo, Kryptonite, that was Ms. Drummond. Put that video on so I can see what you did to her freaky ass. She's ready to get even with Corbin for playing with her emotions."

"Yeah, sometimes you gotta kill a bitch after serving good dick."

"Man, fuck you. I cried when that psychotic bitch sucked my dick," Malakai remembers.

"One question, was it good?"

"Why you think tears were coming from my eyes. I get chills thinking of her crazy ass."

Kryptonite changes the subject. "What's up with Ms. Drummond?"

"You are bringing her to the meeting."

"You sure?"

"If your dick game is what you brag then she will show up with pastries." Malakai erupts with laughter, "Nah, man I'm sure she will be alright. You are picking her up at nine."

Chapter 31

Kryptonite waits patiently for her to arrive at the *Waffle House* parking lot by watching a few hood chicks with bad lace fronts and worn out stilettos.

"Backpage Most Disgusting." he jokes.

He glances at the time displaying 8:50pm. A sudden tap on the windows disrupts his privacy. He looks over and shakes his head. "What the fuck does this ugly bitch want?"

He presses the button to slide the window half-way. "Yes, can I help you?"

"I notice you haven't moved for about 15 minutes and I was wondering what your plans are for tonight," she asks.

"I'm only here for a patty melt, hash browns, and Burt's chili. I'm taking my ass home afterwards."

"My girl and I wouldn't mind accompanying you for the right price this evening," she propositions.

"Young lady, thank you but all I want is my hash browns. By the way, I could be an undercover, and you could easily be arrested."

"You ain't no damn police. You better get the hell out of here before you get robbed."

He reaches down, removes the 9mm, and points at the woman. She throws her hands in the air. "Don't shoot, I was only playing."

"Bitch, you are about to play dead. I don't want your skunky pussy. Get the hell on before I change my mind."

She drops her hands and scurries over to her friends.

"Fucking Malakai got me in this ghetto ass place. Wait until I get back to the cabin."

Her *LX 570* appears; he flashes his lights to signal her towards the corner.

He grabs his belongings and walks to her driver's side. "Slide over, I'm driving."

"What about your car?"

"It's not mine."

She quickly moves and he drives to the cabin. She attempts to breaks the ice. "Is your name really Kevin?"

"Yes, but I never go by that name."

"What shall I call you?"

"Kryptonite. Enough of the chit-chat, I know you want to fuck again. Once you give Malakai the information on your boss, then I'll fuck you senseless."

She coils her tongue and crosses her legs. "I'll give up the world for your dick," she acknowledges.

He shakes his head and thinks *"I'm fucking with a nympho."*

He catches her glancing at him as they travel to their destination. He turns the radio down and asks, "Are you okay?"

She grips her fingers inside of his hand, "I'm thinking how my life has shifted from hunting down Malakai to betraying my boss. Promise me everything will be okay."

"Do what's required and everything will be fine."

"Thank you."

He pulls in the dark pathway and coasts up the gravel road to the cabin. He opens her door and the natural sounds of chirping crickets and hooting owls bring her back to her childhood nights at the trailer park.

"Wow, I haven't heard these sounds in years."

He ignores her enthusiastic demeanor and instructs, "Follow me."

He cradles her arm and leads her to the cabin.

"Welcome to me casa," Malakai greets as he opens the door. "Ms. Drummond, please have a seat. Would you like some coffee, tea, or juice?"

"No, but I would love vodka…straight."

Malakai smiles and responds, "A woman with a nice throat game; I can see why Kryptonite loves you."

He returns minutes later from the bar. "Here you all go."

She takes her drink to the head as soon as it touches her hands. "Whew! That's strong. Do you mind if I stand?"

"Sure, the floor is yours."

"The original paperwork Corbin explained to you at the club is accurate but now there's more. Your flamboyant reputation as a *Poetic Whore* has pissed off a lot of prominent leaders. There's a secret bid for you to serve a life sentence at a maximum prison."

"You shitting me?" Malakai blurts.

She flips her hair over her ear. "No, I'm dead serious."

Kryptonite laughs, "Man, you are going down for slanging dick. I told your crazy ass to come overseas with me."

Malakai scratches his head. "So, if I'm kept alive, what happens to Asperilla?"

She drops her head, "I'm sorry Malakai but he wants her dead; by your hands or his."

Malakai closes his eyes and springs to his feet. "Fuck this, I'm ending it at Corbin's house."

Kryptonite meets him at the door. "I know you are angry, but this is not the way. He is a district attorney and killing him is a death penalty unless they kill you first. Plus, they have your daughter. Sit down, listen, and figure out a new game plan," he suggests.

He thumps Malakai's head. "Use your brain; I taught you better than this. Anytime someone mentions Asperilla's name, you go fucking berserk. I know that's your love but she's not your wife right now. Stay focus."

Malakai calms down. "Yeah, you are right."

He turns to Ms. Drummond, "Is this all the information you have."

"No, he wants to host a party at your club with his own VIP guest list."

Malakai pops his knuckles. "Will Ayanna be there as well?"

"I'm sure she will."

"Great, schedule the party according to his plans."

Kryptonite sees the expression, "I know that look, what are you up to?"

He smiles and pounds Kryptonite's fist, "You told me to think of a new game plan. Let's say I'm about to remove my daughter from his equation."

Chapter 32

"Good Morning Malakai, you haven't called this number in a long time. I was beginning to think you didn't want this sweet pussy anymore," She says.

"I'm sure your juices are dried on the nightstick from our last encounter," he reminds her before laughing.

"Umm. Keep talking dirty so I can play with it." She moans.

"Kim, I need a favor."

"And I need a nut."

"Are you serious? I'm calling you because I need your assistance."

"You can assist with this nut. I'll consider your favor if you make me cum. How fast can you get here?"

He pauses for a second, inserts the key and opens the door. "I'm downstairs, hurry the fuck up," he yells.

Malakai hears heels clacking against the wooden floor.

She stands at the top of the stairwell and announces, "I'm ready."

He tilts his head and peeps out her outfit. She stands naked and grinning from ear to ear. She has on an officer cap and holding a nightstick.

She waves it in the air, "We miss you daddy."

"Kim, I'm married," he mentions and points at his ring.

She smacks her lips. "The whole city knows. What a fucking waste of dick. No woman deserves to have it to herself."

He removes his cufflinks and unbuttons his shirt. "You not getting this dick, but I'll beat the hell out of it."

"I love when you do but you better do a poem. My pussy gets wetter at the sound of your voice."

"Catch! She tosses the nightstick towards him.

He snatches it and arches his eyebrows. "What the hell am I supposed to do with this?"

She glides down the stairs and recommends, "You the poet; use your imagination."

He strips out of his clothes and displays his naked physique.

"Turn around," she commands.

"Mmmm, your ass is still perfect," she moans.

"Yeah, I know. Get on the sofa and spread your legs."

She kisses his cheek, flops on the sofa, and lifts her legs in the air.

"Malakai, on second thought, fuck the poem. Fuck me with the baton. I need to get this nut out quick. Looking at you is good enough."

He slides the baton over her clitoris and gently down the opening of her ass.

She clamps her legs and squeezes the baton. "Damn this feels good."

She opens her legs, leans her head back, and grinds her pussy over the pole.

"Put it in baby, please put it in."

He smiles and ask, "Are you ready?"

"Yes, put it in."

He runs it down one last time before circling the tip of the baton. He jiggles it at the opening of her pussy and eases it in.

Her mouth opens wide but there's no sound. He inserts deeper and she screams.

He wraps his fist tighter around the baton and pushes it in more causing her to lean further back on the couch. She closes her eyes, squeezes her clit with her fingers, and shoves them in her mouth.

"Give me the baton and beat your dick."

He stands over here with his balls hanging in her face. She tugs on them with her teeth, sucks and fucks herself harder.

She releases his balls, "Don't stop stroking."

"Yeah, I'm back and you are the first bitch to catch this nut," he confesses.

She continues harder and cums on the baton and screams at the top of his lungs, "Ahh...ahh...ahh."

"Open your mouth bitch," he commands.

He grabs the back of her head, cums down her throat and it oozes out of her mouth.

She licks the tip, "Umm, it tastes better than I remembered," she recalls.

"Malakai... Malakai... Malakai, I've been calling your name for the past five minutes. What the hell are you doing? How fast can you get here?" she asks.

He snaps out of his wet fantasy, "My bad Kim, I'm already here. I'll meet you downstairs I still have the key you gave me."

He stares at his hard dick and adjust his pants. "Damn, I'm glad I didn't bust a nut thinking about her kinky ass, but that shit felt real as hell," he admits.

He turns the key and walks in the house. She rushes downstairs and jumps in his arms. "Malakai, it has been too long, how's married life?"

"It's wonderful."

She kisses his cheek and responds, "Have a seat and by the way, I was joking earlier. I don't fuck married men."

"Thank God for that."

"What's going on?"

"DA Corbin Lancaster."

"Not the arrogant prick from *Davis Island*. He is corruptive and vindictive. What kind of trouble are you in?"

"Let's say he is out for blood since his crazy girlfriend went missing and blaming my family."

"Is it true?"

"Yep; that bitch had a split personality. One half was in love with him and the other was obsessed with me. She kidnapped me two years ago and tried to kill Asperilla's cousin."

"Malakai, I need a drink because this shit is hilarious."

"It seems everyone thinks the same thing when I mention Nikki's name. Anyway, what do you know about the scandal with the prison systems?"

"It's funny you brought it up. There are rumors floating around the job, but everyone is keeping things on the hush. Let me grab my laptop. Last week I conducted my own investigation of a young male claiming his innocence when drugs were found in his car."

"What type?"

"He had pure unprocessed cocaine in a suitcase."

Malakai shakes his head and answers, "This kind of shit is unheard of in this town; no one is that stupid to transport during the day."

"Umm. I thought the same thing. I brought him in for interrogation. He's a highly respected IT consultant from New York and background is squeaky clean. My gut tells me he was set up."

"What's his name?"

"Antonio Curry."

"Show me a picture."

She clicks on a folder, "Here you go."

Malakai scans the pictures and agrees, "He is not a criminal. What else did you find out about him?"

"He claims he stayed overnight with a female name Ayanna and was pulled over before leaving the neighborhood. He was ready to tell me more until my boss released him to Corbin. I was ordered to leave the room and a few hours later, Antonio walked out a free man. I'm sure they struck a deal."

"Damn, the plot deepens by the moment," Malakai mentions.

She closes the laptop and blurts, "Someone needs to put a stop to his ass. You know he's trying to run for governor in the next election."

"Bullshit!" Malakai yells and grabs his keys, "I gotta run but I need a favor this weekend."

"What do you need?"

"Keep your ears alert for an anonymous tip. When you receive it; follow it."

"Alright, I will. I hope you know what you are doing. Corbin is very dangerous."

"Yeah, but I'm poetic. I'll drop the mic on his punk ass."

Chapter 33

Ayanna walks into the office and finds Ms. Drummond typing speedily. She walks over, bumps the desk and papers whirlwind to the floor.

Ms. Drummond looks up, tilts her glasses, and continues working.

Ayanna was expecting a shady response but didn't receive anything.

She drags a chair in front of her desk, sits down, inhales a deep breath and slurps on her iced vanilla latte loudly to agitate her.

Ms. Drummond stops pecking at the keys but never looks up. "Ayanna, if you don't mind, go to the other office so I can work in peace? No need to get on my damn nerves."

Ayanna leaps from her chair, "Ooh I will tell Corbin you are using profanity in the workplace," she responds in a childish voice.

Ms. Drummond rolls her eyes and speaks softly, "I…don't…care."

Ayanna covers her chest and laughs before responding, "You are becoming a bad bitch."

"Ayanna, the only bad bitch in the room is you."

"That's right. Respect the crown."

Ms. Drummond slides her chair from her desk and crosses her legs. She exhales and speaks with confidence. "Glad you brought up respect. What made you betray Malakai?"

Ms. Drummond's question catches Ayanna off guard, and she isn't sure how to respond.

"No need to answer it; I'm sure it's pure bullshit. I will never forget how you had Corbin drooling over you in the boardroom."

"And he loves every piece of me," she reminds her while groping herself.

Ms. Drummond laughs to herself, "Are you kidding me? Corbin is in love with a fucking corpse. He's a fucking deceiver and his heart belongs to Nikki."

"You are upset he's fucking me instead of your flat ass. Is that's why he's relieving you of your duties after the party."

Ms. Drummond hunch her shoulders and acknowledges, "I guess you will become the new flunky or what they say in your world, the bottom bitch."

She slides her a sealed envelope and demands, "Open it! It's amazing the shit you find with the right connections. How can you betray someone who gave you everything?"

Ayanna scans through the documents and tosses them back to her, "So what, I sold some pussy! I'm sure you sucked some dicks to get where you are today."

Ms. Drummond winks her eye and hints, "You are absolute right, but I never kidnapped a child during the process. I guess you and Corbin are playing house since no man wanted to have kids with you."

Ayanna stands and balls her fist tightly and advises, "Susan, don't say shit about kids to me ever again. This is your only warning."

"Kids!!"

"Stupid bitch!" She yanks her hair and slams her face into the desk.

She elbows Ayanna in the jaw causing her to land on the floor.

"I'm beating your ass," Ayanna promises.

She jumps to her feet and whams her with left and right blows. Ms. Drummond covers up to protect herself and sucker punches Ayanna in the nose. Ayanna is stunned momentarily, and Ms. Drummond claws her neck with her nails.

"I'm fucking you up," Ayanna screams.

She thrusts her hips and tosses Ms. Drummond on the floor. She strikes her repeatedly until someone lifts her in the air. She turns around and screams at the security guard. "Let me go! I'm not done with her ass. You a dead bitch when I see you again," She screams while being dragged by security.

Ms. Drummond stands and dusts her clothes. Her office looks like a tornado has swept through with chairs turned over and trash everywhere. She squats and grabs the purse from under the desk. She reaches inside and pulls out her compact mirror. Her face is swollen from the fight. She smiles for the first time in months and proud of herself for standing up to her. She closes the mirror, opens a word document and begins typing:

"Subject: Susan Drummonds - Resignation

Dear Mr. Corbin Lancaster:

This is to formally notify you that I am terminating myself as your assistance district attorney effective immediately.

I appreciate the professional training, social and personal development opportunities I've had. Thank for also making me feel like shit since you started fucking Ayanna. I hope you and your bitch rot in hell with your precious Nikki.

Best Regards,

Susan Drummonds"

She proofreads, attaches it to an email and chuckles while clicking the send button.

She boxes her important work, grabs her favorite plant, and flips the light switch off. She reminisced one last time over the good and horrible days. She walks pass the security guard and acknowledges, "Thanks for your help Joe."

"No problem ma'am, it's my job. I'll carry those things to your car."

"You don't have too."

"No, I assist."

They walk toward the elevator and he stirs up a conversation, "I contacted Mr. Lancaster and he asked me to escort Ayanna from the premises. So where are you going?"

She smiles and answers, "To start my path on becoming a District Attorney.

He presses the elevator button and extends his hands. "Ladies first."

The door closes and they ride to the parking garage. He walks her to the car and ensures she is safe. "Well, that's everything and if you need anything don't forget to call me."

She smiles and responds, "Joe, if I didn't think any better; I would think you are flirting with me."

"No ma'am, just doing my job."

She gives him a hug and thanks him for assisting. Joe closes the door and she drives through the parking deck. She made it to the freeway and the burner cell rings.

She reaches into the console and answers, "Hello."

"Are you ok?"

"Yes, but she is vicious. I thought she was going to kill me especially when I mentioned the baby. She's beyond crazy."

"Yeah, I love gutty women. You should leave town until this is over."

"Can Kryptonite come?"

He chuckles and responds, "You can ask him yourself."

"Okay, I will talk to him later. Malakai, you are alright in my book. Thanks for the help and I'll call you another time."

She ends the call and blushes about Kryptonite as she drives home.

Chapter 34

Ayanna approaches the gate and holds down the horn nonstop until the guard appears. She stomps on the gas pedal once the gate opens and speeds to the mansion. She ignores the security team as she storms inside, tosses her bags and releases a loud scream.

Ms. Garcia runs from the kitchen with her a finger over her lips. "Señorita Ayanna, can you keep your voice down, Graciana is sleeping," she whispers.

"Fuck that little Gremlin. I'll scream as loud as I want. This is my damn house. Umm, you might be on to something. After the day I had, peace is something I deserve.

She dashes upstairs and Ms. Garcia runs behind her yelling, "Parada! Parada!"

Ayanna grabs a pillow from her bedroom and proclaims, "I'll suffocate that fucking monster."

She attempts to grab it but her small frame is no match. Ayanna hears the baby laughing down the hall. Her adrenaline increases from the thought of killing Asperilla's only child. She pushes Ms. Garcia to the floor and sprints to the nursery. She kicks in the door and her mouth drops when she sees Asperilla with her feet propped up playing with her.

She tickles her feet and confirms, "Gracy, it's your Auntie Ayanna. Don't worry about remembering her face, she won't be around long enough to see your first birthday."

Ayanna huffs and puffs. "Dammit! Can my day get any worse? Why the fuck are you here?"

"The question is where were you going with the pillow?"

"To put your daughter to sleep; forever."

"What's stopping you?"

"Fuck you Asperilla, your day is coming."

"Same thing Christians say about Jesus."

Asperilla phone chimes with a text, "It looks like Corbin is on his way home. Make sure you ask him why I'm here."

Ayanna's lips quiver as she attempts to speak, "You know what Asper-?"

"Bitch keep my name out your mouth," Asperilla blurts out. "You are fucking lucky Corbin has security."

Asperilla points toward the door. "Get the hell out! You are ruining my moments with my daughter."

"I'll go for now but remember you aren't dealing with the old me," Ayanna warns while walking out the door.

She goes to the bar and finds something to drink. Her whole day has been fucked up and needs something strong to soothe the evening. She flips through the cabinet and select some Hennessy. *"This shit will do."*

She pours a glass, mixes it with coke and guzzles it down. She closes her eyes and pauses for a second.

The front door opens, and Corbin kisses her like he does every day. She leans her head back to avoid his advances. "Oh, hell no, I'm too pissed for romance. First, it was Ms. Drummond and now it's Asperilla."

She mixes another one, takes a sip and sits the glass down. "Explain to me why she is upstairs?""

He grabs her hand and explains, "Listen, I know you hate Asperilla, but we need her."

She snatches away and confirms, "Get the fuck off me because my plan was flawless. You, Ms. Drummond and

Asperilla can kiss my ass. For the record Corbin, I don't need that bitch."

"Yes, you do," Asperilla interrupts from the stairwell. "You have always needed me, and your boss does too. I don't trust ya'll shady muthafuckers but I'm here to help."

Asperilla glances at Ayanna, 'Sit your ass down and listen. I know you want the business and you can have it. For years, I have thought about killing Malakai for fucking all those women. I once hired a hit man but called it off after he decided to be faithful. Now as for you Ayanna, your plan was all right, but you have no idea how he thinks."

"And you do?" Ayanna responds.

"He'll drop his guard around me, and Corbin knows I'm the only sure thing to get close to him."

"Ladies join me at the table and combine our resources to take out the common enemy," he suggests.

They take a seat and Corbin speaks, "Asperilla, if you cross me; I will make sure your precious daughter is sold as a sex slave throughout the four corners of the earth. I'll send you weekly pictures while you rot in a Mexican outhouse."

"I love that idea," Ayanna says.

Asperilla smiles in her direction and responds, "Humph, I'm sure you did with your trifling ass. I won't fail but I'm tired of you ordering me around. You have a slick tongue and think you are untouchable but never use a woman-child as collateral. There's a monster inside of every mother. I'll kill Malakai but not until my baby is safe."

Corbin nods in acknowledgement, "You have my word." He extends his hands to seal the deal.

"I don't shake hands with the devil," she revolts and slaps his hand away. "Our meeting is over; I'll contact you when I have him."

Ayanna snickers to herself as she walks away.

Asperilla turns around and says, "You are really pressing my nerves, little girl. You keep yapping and see what happens."

"Not a damn thing, you ain't doing shit with your baby upstairs."

Corbin sees Asperilla going in her purse and hints, "Don't do anything you will regret."

She ignores him and continues searching.

Corbin snaps his fingers and two men with weapons draw on Asperilla.

She never looks up, chuckles and shakes her head. "Relax, it's only lipstick plus they searched me when I came in."

They place their weapons in the holsters and return to their post by the door.

"They should have searched your stretched-out pussy; no telling what's hiding in there," Ayanna reveals.

Asperilla drops her purse, leaps across the table and swings the lipstick inches from her neck.

Ayanna laughs and responds, "I keep telling you I'm not the old me. You don't scare me anymore."

Asperilla returns to her seat and proclaims, "Bitch, I wasn't trying to scare you; only a reminder how quick death comes."

"With lipstick? Get the fuck out of here with that shit."

Asperilla tosses the lipstick on the table.

Ayanna gasps after seeing a 1 & 1/4" stainless steel blade from the tip.

"I thought you searched her," Corbin yells.

"We did sir," they respond.

Asperilla smiles at Ayanna and says, "Death comes quickly to bitches who talk shit."

She claps her heels, spins around, and looks at Corbin, "Now I can leave."

Chapter 35

Mei and Meiying skip to the cabin holding hands and singing, "We're going to kill some people; bloody, bloody people."

Malakai hears the commotion outside and runs to open the door. "What the hell are ya'll so jolly about?"

They stare at each other quietly. "Should I tell him, or do you want to do it?" Mei asks.

"Just spit it out," He yells in an irritable voice.

"Alright, the bug Ms. Drummond placed on Ayanna led us to a waterfront mansion in St. Pete. It's in the middle of nowhere and heavily guarded with security," Mei explains.

"Do you think we can get my daughter out of there alive?"

"Yea, but you need to listen to the audio," Meiying suggests.

"Give me everything and I will meet up with you all later."

Mei tosses the surveillance and skips away with Meiying.

His stomach tightens as the sound of Asperilla's voice. *"What the fuck is she doing there?"*

He snatches the earpiece and says, "You're a treacherous bitch. I'll suck the last breath out of your soul."

He goes into the den with the family and says, "It's time to fuck up something and I don't care whose blood you spill. Get my damn daughter!"

"I'm about killing everything that moves but what about the diversion," Mei reminds him.

He smiles in her direction before speaking, "No worries, Corbin is planning a party at Love Divine's with his elite friends. I have a friend but she won't be able to hold him long so this must be quick and precise. There's a stockpile of guns and ammunition in the storage tunnel; feel free to grab whatever you need.

He pulls his keys out of his pocket and says, "I'll return later. I'm going to visit an old friend."

"You know you want to eat her pussy one last time. You aren't fooling us," Kryptonite jokes.

"Whatever man, I'm not going near her ass, least… not tonight."

He leaves the house to visit Love Divine's gravesite. He snaps his fingers and sings as he drives. Half of the playlist is completed by the time he reaches the cemetery. He grabs his gun and makes sure he isn't being followed. He creeps through the eerie path and makes his way to her tombstone.

"Divine, I'm here again. Yeah, I know it has been a minute and I was hoping I didn't have to come back. I traveled the world when my daughter was born. We ended up living in Africa for a while. I knew you would have loved it. You should have seen the beautiful Motherland. Oh my God, it was incredible."

He exhales and wipes his face, "I already know what you are about to ask. Why am I here? Asperilla was homesick and I sacrificed my family. I'm not worrying about the mess with Corbin, I didn't even fuck his bit-. My bad, I meant to say I never had sexual relations with his woman. I went the faithful route. *Except when Nikki sucked the skin off my dick.*"

He feels a grim chill running through his soul from reminiscing about that moment. "Ahem, sorry about that, where was I? Yeah, I was faithful, and it wasn't hard as I thought. My poetry is well, and I perform occasionally but it's not the same since you aren't around. I wish you could have met my daughter. She has a gorgeous smile with my eyes and Asperilla's complexion and hair. She will be a handful for these fellas in the future."

He whispers a silent prayer, stoops down, and kisses the entrance to her resting place.

"Love Divine, my time is up. I'll bring something special on my return."

He returns to his car. The mere thought of her has driven him to not lose another woman. He pushes the ignition button and pulls out the cemetery.

He drives back to the house listening to soft music. *This Woman's Work* by *Maxwell* comes on and is Asperilla's favorite making love song. He thinks of their first date, marriage, and the birth of Graciana. He's not ready to lose it all because of Corbin's stipulations. He waits until the song finishes playing and calls Asperilla. He wasn't sure if she would answer but he needs to hear her voice. The ringing stops and his heart flutters from anticipation.

"Buenas tardes Malakai," she answers.

"Good Evening Asperilla, how are you?"

"I'm wonderful; sitting hear painting my toes red and wishing it was your blood.

He exhales before engaging her wicked thoughts. "I'm working on a plan. You don't have to team up with Corbin."

"Umm, I like the idea of bringing your head. This is your fucking fault Malakai."

"Your love for poetry destroyed our family and you will pay. Graciana and I will be fine without you. Please make sure you kiss Isabella tonight because I'm slicing her head off as well."

"Asperilla, you are talking crazy. What the fuck is wrong with you?"

"Are you serious? You are my problem. I gave you a moment of comfort at the hotel before I issued your death sentence." She laughs with evilness.

"Asperilla!!"

"I'm here baby. I will send a present this week to show my love. You will appreciate me for doing it."

"Humph! This call isn't getting us anywhere. Keep your damn present. I was only calling to see if we could salvage this marriage. We have been through worse but I'm not dying by your hands."

"I agree; you won't die by my hands, but my knife is a different story. When it is all done, I will drink your blood to celebrate."

"You won't change Asperilla. I'm tired of asking."

His tone changes from sincere to demanding. "Pack your bags tonight; leave town and don't return until I tell you."

"I'm not going no damn where," she snaps back.

She yawns through the phone then whispers, "Look, you are boring me. Sueños sangrientos."

The call drops and the radio returns to the previous song. "Damn, that hardheaded bitch hung up on me."

Chapter 36

Monique stands by the bar with arms folded and watches Corbin flaunts as the new owner.

He whistles for the bartender's attention, "Another round of drinks for my special guests," he announces.

The bartender gives Monique a puzzling look.

"Go ahead and fix anything he needs," she replies.

The bartender steps away and prepares the drinks.

"What's wrong Monique, you don't enjoy the way I'm running things in my club. "

"Corbin, this club is not yours and I'll be damned if I put up with your shit because you are blackmailing Malakai."

He chuckles and leans toward her ear. "Bitch, you'll be serving from your knees by the time I'm done with you."

"Your friends are wannabe gangstas with law books. You don't scare me, and I'll never work for or with you. Drink up tonight… Drink it all because Malakai will pour liquor on the ground for you and your goons."

She attempts to walk away but he yanks her wrist. "I'm not done talking to you. Yeah, I know the law and know Malakai won't do shit but serve time for illegal activity."

He releases her wrist. "Hoe go play. I'm sure he has taught you the meaning."

She swings her hands in the direction of his face. He catches and squeezes his fingers around hers. She didn't flinch or grimace. He releases and pushes her away.

"Here are your drinks Mr. Corbin," the bartender interrupts.

He sips and winks at the bartender. "Young lady, you are getting a raise tonight."

He tilts his glass towards Monique, "Act right or die wrong, it's your choice."

"Whatever Corbin, you can head back to the VIP section; someone will serve your table," she assures.

"That's more like it."

He joins the rest of his group.

"What took you so long?" Ayanna asks.

"I was getting acquainted with Monique. I like her style and could be a great asset to the team."

"Corbin, you are becoming overconfident each day. I hope you not putting my life on the line with these childish games."

"Relax Ayanna, I remembered you being the one with the ego when you walked in my office."

He kisses her cheek and presses his thumb against her chin, "Tonight is our time to celebrate plus Asperilla promises to take care of Malakai tonight."

The bartender arrives and set the drinks in front of them. She accidentally spills red wine on Ayanna's white blouse.

Ayanna jumps from her seat screaming, "You're a clumsy bitch, you ruined my damn outfit."

"Baby, I'll buy you one tomorrow. Let's enjoy our new club."

Ayanna points her finger at the bartender's face, "Bitch, today is your lucky day."

"Corbin, I have to get this stain out. I'll be right back." She fusses and runs to the restroom.

Monique watches everything and follows behind. She approaches Ayanna at the sink as she unbuttons her blouse. "Why are you doing this?"

Ayanna laughs and responds, "Wow another one of Malakai's loyal followers. I'm sure he loves the way you manages this club."

She fans her blouse and turns, "To be honest, it's not Malakai at all; I hate his fucking wife. Instead of questioning me, you should be terminating your sorry ass employee for spilling wine."

Monique takes a step back and responds, "I apologize for her actions and will do as you wish."

She walks away and leaves Ayanna inside the restroom. She locks it and chats with an unknown female wearing a masquerade mask. "Are you ready to do this?"

"Hell yeah!" she exclaims.

"That's the answer I was expecting. Corbin is sitting in the VIP section. He's all yours for the moment."

"No worries, I'll have his dick exploding within minutes."

Monique leaves the woman, strolls to the DJ booth and whispers in his ear. He mutes the music and announces, "Attention in the club, attention in the club. Tonight, we are taking it up a level for our new owner Corbin Lancaster. Show him what it means to be Love Divine."

The crowd raises their glasses and echoes the phrase, "Love is divine and divine is love."

The lights dim and Corbin's security rushes to his section.

The DJ spins *Only If You're Tippin* by *Campfire*. The mysterious masked woman steps out wearing thigh boots and a trench coat. She unties the belt and drop it to the floor modeling a red satin bow teddy with halter and shoulder straps. The slim straps underneath the flirty bow design drapes from her rib cage, down her stomach, and covers her jewels.

She rotates and showcases her adjustable strappy thong sliding up her ass. She dances with her eyes locked on Corbin.

He licks his lips as she approaches and notices her similarities to Nikki. His dick pulsates from thinking of their past lovemaking.

She smiles, turns around, and touch her toes viewing her beautiful yellow ass. She jiggles her cheeks and claps them together. She reaches her arms through her inner thighs, massages them, and slides her hands down to her calf muscles. Her legs widen displaying flexibility and sexiness. She bounces up, turns around, and steps closer. She grabs his hands and places them on her breasts.

He closes his eyes for a moment and glides his hand over her breast as he was turning the steering wheel of his *Phantom Rolls-Royce*.

She licks her lips, throws his hands away, falls to her knees, and glides her ass on the heels of her boots. She repeats the movement while blowing kisses at him.

Her ass resembles two gigantic peaches. She eases down and sits in a reverse position on his lap. She flips her hair, grinds over his chest, and he loves every minute.

"Corbin get off that bitch, I know you're not disrespecting me," Ayanna says.

He pushes her off and responds, "Not at all…Just having a little fun."

He fixes his shirt and asks, "Where have you been?"

"Someone locked me in the restroom but fuck that. Get off my man, bitch!" She shouts.

The masked woman smiles, lifts off Corbin, and dances on Ayanna.

She pushes her down and the woman tumbles and dances on the floor.

Everyone thinks it is a part of her routine. The masked woman stands to her feet, lifts her left leg vertically in the air, and points her fingers at Ayanna.

The DJ stops the music as the lights come on and Ayanna recognizes the woman standing in front of her.

"Jaz, what are you doing here?"

She removes her mask and gives a revengeful smile. Ayanna is moments away from tackling Jaz when the police rush through the doors. A female detective steps through the crowd flashing her badge to the VIP section, "Corbin Lancaster, we have reports of illegal drug distributions and prostitution in this establishment."

He takes a sip of his drink before responding, "Detective, you have no idea who I am. I will have your head. What's your badge number?"

"The only thing I'm giving is a ride downtown."

One of his security guards recognize the detective and whispers something in his ear.

He calms down and responds, "Okay lead the way."

Corbin follows her through the crowd, stopping suddenly to speak with Ayanna, "Activate the plan, I know Malakai is behind this."

Ayanna responds, "Do I need to follow you?"

"Yes, meet me at the station but tell Monique I'm burning this club to the ground."

The officers turn around. "Mr. Lancaster, please follow me."

He kisses Ayanna's cheek and exits through the crowd.

She searches for Jaz, blows her frustrations out her nostrils and mumbles, "I will get you for this."

She pulls out her phone and her skin crawls after seeing the number in her contacts. She honors Corbin's wishes and press the call button. "Asperilla, do it tonight."

"Gladly," she responds.

Ayanna presses end and watches everyone evacuate the club. She thinks to herself, *"Damn, I hope we won't be at the police station all morning."*

Chapter 37

Mei and Meiying lie in the bushes outside of Corbin's property.

Meiying drops the binoculars and checks her watch. "Where is Malakai? "

Mei hunches her shoulders and responds, "I'm giving him five more minutes before we do things our way."

Malakai's sexy voice comes through their headsets. "Relax ladies, I'm here, I was buying some time. Now let's do this shit quickly."

"Roger that," Meiying acknowledges.

Mei stands and cracks her neck and knuckles. "You ready sis?"

Meiying chambers her first round through her semi-automatic *AR-15 rifle*. "Let's blow off some dicks."

Mei scoops down and lifts her *RPG launcher* on her shoulder, adjusts her optical sight, closes her left eye and aims for the security post. She inhales for a second, releases, and squeezes the trigger. The rocket whistles through the air. The fiery blaze alerts the security teams and they run out the house armed.

Meiying squeezes the trigger and mows them down instantly giving Mei enough time to load another *RPG*.

Mei aims directly at the front door and launches the rocket toward the guards. It explodes, as they watch the guards jump off the porch and hide behind the cars.

Meiying speaks through her headset, "Malakai, we can hold them. You gotta go now."

"On it."

He takes advantage of the diversion, jumps the gate behind the house and rushes toward the back door.

He peeps through the window and sees two guards by the door. He pulls out his 9mm silencer, knocks on the door and falls to the ground.

As the guard opens the door, Malakai fires two rounds from his back. The bullets penetrate through their heads. One body drops backward and the other one fell on Malakai.

He rolls the body. "Oomph, get the fuck off!"

He leaps to his feet and runs in the house. He pauses behind the corner and sees the coast is clear.

Mei reminds him, "Malakai, hurry the fuck up the police will be here soon."

"Aight," he replies.

"Upstairs or down, where will I keep a hostage," he thinks.

"Basement," he mumbles.

He will make sure to kiss Ms. Drummond for the blueprints. He slides a book bag under the kitchen table, rushes through the den, and creep downstairs. He turns the corner with his weapons drawn on the guard, "Don't move and don't say shit."

The guard freezes and follows his orders.

"Are they in there?"

"Who?"

Malakai shoots his groin and he falls with his hands between his thighs.

He kicks the guard in the face, "Bitch, give me the code to the door and the rear gate. Don't make me ask twice."

"1.9.8.5," he grunts.

Malakai punches the code and the door opens. He stares at the guard and shoots him in the head.

He pulls out a zip-lock bag, knife, and takes home a souvenir. He enters the basement and finds a Hispanic woman crouched in the corner holding Graciana.

He waves the lady over and she hesitates for a second.

"Soy su padre. Ven conmigo," he translates.

The lady runs over and gives him a hug. He peels the blanket to his beautiful daughter smiling.

He knows his daughter is cursed with Asperilla emotions, *"Who the hell smiles during a fight?"*

He scans the room for the trap door to outside. He grabs the woman's hands and leads her behind the bookcase. He flips the *Art of War* backwards and the walls open to the left.

"Ms. Drummond, I appreciate the second tip," he mutters.

They rush through and it seals quickly behind them. They continue to the stairwell and out the door. He barely opens it and steps out first to ensure the scene is safe. He waves his hand to her and she follows closely. They lock hands and sprint to the back gate.

He taps the code and the gate opens. They quickly run to the parked van.

Kryptonite and Isabella stand outside armed and ready to take out anything coming their way.

Malakai speaks into the headset. "Ladies, you all can move out. Graciana is safe."

"Easy for you; they are pinning us. Do something!" Mei yells.

Malakai pulls out his phone and dials a number to the bomb in the bookbag. He watches the explosion.

"It worked; they are turning around," Mei yells.

"Ok, meet us at the rally point," Malakai says.

"Copy that!"

He gets in the van, "Let's go because you can only hold a district attorney for a short time."

They drive the back road and picks up the twins. They hop in and tears stream down Mei's eyes.

"Meiying, what's up with your sister?" Malakai asks.

"She's disappointed because she didn't claim a trophy."

Malakai reaches into his jacket pocket and tosses her the ziplock bag.

She catches it and her eyes and mouth widens. "Wow! This is some *John Holmes* shit," she exclaims.

She pulls out the dick and waves it in the air. "I got a trophy; thank you Malakai."

"No problem. You deserve it."

Malakai wipes his forehead and grateful everyone made it out with no injuries. "Thank you all for helping me get my daughter. There's no way I could have done it without you, "he acknowledges.

"That's what family is for," Kryptonite says.

"Yeah, we love you," Mei adds.

"More than your trophy piece?"

"Not quite but close. "

"Isabella, you did well," Malakai speaks with appreciation.

"I was ready to shoot, especially since I've been training," Isabella says.

"In time you will. Let's go home and rest," He recommends.

He closes his eyes, leans his head against the seat, and enjoys a moment of peace. He wakes up when the van stops at the cabin. They unload and prepare for tomorrow's adventure.

Malakai enters the cabin and rushes to the shower. He pounds his fist against the wall and never wanted to return to a monster but Corbin and Asperilla left him no choice.

He finishes his shower, dress, and checks on Graciana.

He knocks on the door, "Isabella, it's me," he confirms.

"Come in," she answers.

He walks to the other side of the bed. "Aww, she's asleep. I was looking forward to sharing an evening with her."

"Do you want her," Isabella ask?

"No, I'll play with her in the morning."

He closes the door and walks to his room knowing he can finally get a good night's sleep with half of his family.

Chapter 38

Malakai phone rings in the wee hours of the morning. He retrieves it and sees Asperilla's number.

"Why the hell she's calling me at 3:30 am," he mumbles and tosses the phone.

It rings five minutes later. He jumps, throws a pillow, and snatches it. "What the fuck do you want?"

"Mmmm, yell at me again. My pussy gets wetter from anger. If you listen, you can hear her dripping your name."

"Asperilla, why are you playing on my phone? Didn't I ask you to leave town and not return until I send for you?"

"Send for me? God can't send for me. You have lost your fucking mind. Since you love sending shit, how do you want your bitch?"

"What the fuck are you talking about? I don't have time for this shit."

He ends the call and turns over. He sleeps a full hour until the phone chimes with nonstop text messages. He grabs and takes it to the bathroom. Standing over the toilet, he swipes the phone and a picture of Love Divine's gravesite is displayed.

"Ah, Shit!" He pisses on the floor after seeing the tombstone broken in half.

The next picture has her name scratched off and replaced with Asperilla's name and the caption reads, "I'm the only bitch who loves you; not these dead hoes."

He dials her number and shouts, "Bitch, you have gone too far."

Asperilla laughs through the phone and jokes, "My pussy is gushing, call me another bitch."

"You are a dumb bitch; wait until I get my hands on you."

"Ooh, I'm scared. I need a nut to squirt my juices over her grave then the windows of heaven will open. Hallelujah!"

"When I see you, I'm choking you to sleep."

"One dead body down, another one to dig up. If you want me; come and get me," she teases and hangs up.

He rushes out the bedroom with his clothes, turns the corner and bump heads with Kryptonite.

"Where the hell are you going this time of the morning?" He asks.

"Unfinished business with my wife."

"Man don't freeze when you see her. I'll make preparation for Graciana and Isabella."

"You act like I'm not coming back. I can handle her."

Kryptonite places his hand over his mouth to cover his yawn, "Whatever Malakai; we'll keep her from your daughter. I'm going back to bed."

Malakai dashes to his car and drives to Nikki's unmarked grave to meet his wife. He rides in silent for an hour in a half, praying he could reason with her one last time. He drives until the pavement turns to gravel, bears left, and parks at the old campground.

He grabs his gun, mini flashlight, and proceeds to the cabin. He shakes his head and questions his life, "Why can't I be a normal poet with a family and run a nightclub?"

He approaches the cottage with the element of surprise. The windows are boarded with grass and weeds around the path.

The memories of being held hostage lingers in his soul. He shivers and shrugs his shoulders, "I hate this place. Once I finish Corbin off then it will be demolished."

He marches until he sees a gigantic oak tree. He aims his pistol and tiptoes toward her remains. He overhears rustling in the bushes, pauses his steps, and lowers to the ground. He keeps his head up and sees a dark figure.

He would have fired but decides to take a softer approach. He slides the knife from the sheath and slitters toward the direction of the voices. The moon and stars provide enough visual to sneak behind the first guy.

"Hey, you guys go ahead, I'll catch up in a few I have to piss," the masculine voice states.

He eases closer and hears the wetness on the bushes. *"I hope he doesn't piss on my face."*

He clutches the handle of the knife, leaps up, and wrestles the man to the ground before slicing his throat. He ponders how many are waiting for him and where is Asperilla?

He is 100 feet away from the grave site and hears a muzzling sound. He shines his light and discovers Asperilla gagged and tied to a tree. A piece of him wants to leave her but his devotion overrules her treachery. He stands to his feet and walks in her directions. She mumbles louder, alerting there's another intruder.

He puts his gun away, unties her and removes the gag. "You ok baby?" He asks.

She releases a soft sigh and nods in compliance.

A white male appears from the bushes with his weapon drawn on Malakai. "Keeps your hands up."

"So, this is the big bad Malakai; you aren't all that," a white male discloses.

Malakai steps closer until Asperilla's breath is against his neck.

"Take another step and your body will be in her grave."

"What's your name?" Malakai asks.

"That's not important. Shut the hell up!"

Malakai laughs loudly.

"What's so funny?" The white male inquires.

"Death is here, and you are too stupid to notice," Malakai responds.

Asperilla grabs the *Glock 42* from Malakai's rear holster, pushes him down and fires two shots in his head.

His body drops, "Damn, I didn't get his name," Malakai jokes.

"I knew you couldn't betray me baby."

"Oh, but I am," she responds and injects a needle in the side of his neck.

He turns and wraps his hands around her neck, but the dose is working quickly. He loosens his grip and falls to his knees.

She kisses his lips and knocks him on the head with the gun and his body wobbles to the ground. She grabs the shovel behind the tree and slams the blade inches away from his head. "Never trust a bitch with a booty and smile."

She calls Corbin but his phone goes to voicemail and pisses her off.

She screams into the phone, "Malakai's down, give me my fucking baby!!!"

Chapter 39

Malakai opens his eyes in darkness with a throbbing headache. He shortens his breath and focuses on how good pussy has caused his downfall. A cool breeze under his balls means he is naked.

He attempts to move from his position but and his body swings back and forward. He cannot move his hands or feet. He is hogtied and suspended in the air.

He remembers this position well from his *Poetic Whore* days. He used to fuck with a dominatrix and loved dangerous and kinky shit. His flashback was short lived as the door creeps open by the sound of two male voices.

The first voice speaks to the second one, "Pull the bag off that nigga and let's see if he's breathing."

The second one lowers him waist level, unties and slides the bag off.

Malakai inhales the fresh air but remains silent with his eyes closed. He mentally recites carnal sin number one. *"Never let your enemy exploit your weakness."*

The first assailant picks up a bucket of water and splashes his face. "Wake your bitch ass up," he shouts!

Malakai shakes the water off, opens his eyes and stares, "Get Corbin's bitch ass. I'm not playing these kiddie games."

They laugh at his demands and the first assailant drops the bucket and slaps his face, "You can't order anyone around. What the fuck we look like, one of your hoes? Oh, I forgot you don't have them."

The other assailant punches him in the face and exclaims, "That's for fucking my wife."

Malakai laughs and responds with a smart comment, "If that's how you hit, no wonder she gave up the ass."

He balls his fist harder to swing again but the first assailant stops him. "Don't waste your time on this idiot, we have big plans for him. Get the boss and maybe it's time to put his mangy ass to sleep…permanently," he says.

The second assailant places the bag over his head and walks out the room.

Malakai knows he can't stay in this position and needs a way to escape. He overhears loud clacking from the hallway. The smell of a Cuban cigar lingers followed by irritating and screeching sounds like fingernails scratching a chalkboard; then the noise halts below him. The second assailant snatches the bag off his head.

Sitting in a chair is a woman in a ski mask with a dark skirt, white blouse and a pair of black stretched *Gianvito* ankle boots. She puffs on her cigar and blows the smoke in his face.

He coughs a few times and turns his head to avoid the smell.

She snatches his chin and sink her nails deep until blood slides through her fingers. She places the tip of her finger in her mouth and sucks his blood greedily.

Her familiar *Dolce & Gabbana* scent drifts under his nose. He lifts his head and winks, "You are wearing my favorite perfume," he acknowledges.

She smiles as he discovers she is here to end his life. Pulls off the mask to reveal her beautiful face and asks, "Did you miss me Malakai?"

He refuses to answer which aggravates her. She sinks her nails deeper. "Continue to be silent and you won't have a tongue."

He responds in a sluggish tone, "Death is better than being betrayed by the woman you love. Kill me!"

"I plan on it. I refuse to lose my baby over your bullshit. I will rip out your heart and eat our love away."

She snaps her fingers and the second assailant runs over, "Bring his surprise present and hurry up," she demands.

He dashes out the room and returns within three minutes. He drops the bag and asks with servitude, "Anything else boss?"

"No that will be all, please exit the room. You all might not want to see what's about to happen."

Now she knows he is all to herself. "Is poetry your first love? You don't have to answer. Hell, the world knows it and it's one of the reasons you don't have me."

She slaps his face and screams, "Bitch that's for our daughter."

She swings her legs backward and kicks him in the abdomen multiples times. He tightens his abs and sustains the blows. She wipes the sweat from her brow, squats by his ear and whispers, "You are one selfish asshole."

"You can kiss my selfish ass. After all I've done for you and this is my payment; you never loved me."

She licks her lips and says, "Baby, I loved you to death and your last breath will escape between my thighs.

She walks to her bag and pulls out his personal gold-plated microphone with *The Poetic Whore* engraved on the handle. She waves it in the air and yells, "Mic check one… mic check two. I'm not sure it's working. Maybe it needs to be connected to the power source."

She spreads her legs, slides the mic under her skirt, and massages her clit. She moans heavily as her juices trickle down her leg.

He watches the single stream from her vagina to her thigh.

She snatches the mic and plunges the head in his mouth. "Suck on this; taste my juices."

She shoves the mic deeper to see him gag. "I hate your ass," she screams. "No, I take that back, I love you."

She pulls lubrication out the bag and massages his ass cheeks before penetrating her fingers into his asshole. "Since poetry is a part of you. I'm dropping the mic deep… deep… deep to feel every inch; all of them."

"Asperilla, I'm not playing with you, cut this shit out!!"

"Now you want to speak? Alright, I'll stop but let me ask you something. How does it feel to be powerless? Never mind, don't bother but you will eat me one last time before you die," she notifies.

She hikes her skirt, grabs his head and face fucks him. Her pussy juices drip from the corner of his mouth.

She grabs the rope and thrusts his face. "Tell me you miss me. Tell me, who owns your face, Tell me! "she yells.

She grinds and grunts ferociously, "You will drown in this pussy."

Malakai tries to shift his face but has limited movement. He attempts to fight but surrenders to her sweetness. He sucks and tugs on her lips praying she has a change of heart after her orgasm.

He burrows and twists his tongue, biting her clit and sucking her juices.

"I love your mouth."

Asperilla hears a knock on the door and screams, "Go away."

The knocks are louder and faster. She pushes his face away, pulls her skirt down and pulls the pink revolver from her bag.

She storms to the door with her revolver aimed and swings it open. "What do you want? You fucked up my nut."

"Understood but Corbin needs to speak with you right away," the assailants inform.

"Damn, ya'll men are all the same; can't do shit right! Stay here and watch him," she instructs.

She turns and winks, "I'll be back to finish and place two bullets in your head."

She giggles at her humorous statement, claps her heels and walks out the room.

Chapter 40

In the mist of sucking and tugging on her clit, Malakai was able to loosen the knot around his wrists. Unfortunately, the rope is around his ankles, but he has a plan.

He had stared at the machete against the wall since they pulled the bag off his head. His only option is to get close to reach it. If he fails, Corbin wins, and he will be sold to the highest bidder.

"Fuck that," he thinks.

He looks at the assailant for a minute and asks, "What is your wife's name?"

"You should know. You fucked her."

"Bro, no disrespect but I have fucked plenty of women. It's clear your wife wasn't special, or I would have remembered."

He knows the plan is working as he talks shit and sliding his hand through the rope.

"Maybe you can tell me about her mouth game, I'm a sucker for oral. I never forget a woman who deep throats and scrapes me with her teeth."

"I'm tired of your shit. Don't make me kill you before Corbin does."

He gets relentless and tosses another insult, "I bet you loved kissing your wife after she guzzled my cock juice. You come home tasting my leftover poetry on her lips. Hell, you should pay me for getting her in the mood to fuck your worthless ass. She told me how you couldn't last two minutes in the sheets."

"I'm going to skin your black ass alive."

Malakai laughs from his lies leaving him dumbfounded and upset. His hands are free and rocks to gain momentum. He predicts he will charge him. He just need one more insult to throw him off guard. He rocks harder, swinging back and forth. He keeps his hands behind his back, tightens his left fist and throws his last insult, "When you get home tonight take a good look at your son because he probably has my eyes."

Malakai swings backward once the assailant charges him. He uppercuts him in the balls, dangles over him, and grabs the machete. He shreds the rope connected to the cable ring above him praying it's enough time to free himself before the assailant recovers.

He saws the rope, dropping him to the floor. He presses his chest flat, lifts his legs upward, and contorts them over his head. He shreds through the rope and loosen his bound ankles. "Whew, flexibility and yoga have saved my life."

He removes the ropes, picks up the machete, and stands over him. "You never have to question another man about your wife again," he confirms while slicing his head with the machete.

He swings again, "This is for punching me in the face," until blood splats on his naked chest.

He smiles after delivering the final blow. He steps over the body and walks toward the door with the machete dripping a trail of blood. He waits patiently for Asperilla or the other assailant. A few minutes later, he hears screaming and the running of footsteps toward the room, "They have the baby!!"

The door opens and Malakai swings the machete and slashes the assailant wrist causing him to drop the gun.

"Fuck," the assailant screams.

Malakai picks up the weapon and aims at his head, "Where's Asperilla?"

"Down the hall," he groans.

"Get your ass up and walk."

He stalls by the doorway, but Malakai presses the machete blade against his throat. "Let's go before I shove it through the back of your neck."

He staggers along the hallway until they reach the office. Malakai places a single finger over his lip. He waves the gun toward the door and motions for him to knock. He kicks the door and quickly falls to the floor. From inside the office, a bullet is fired shattering the glass and lodging inside the wall.

"Drop the weapon Asperilla and end this shit," Malakai yells.

"You never give up. I should have shot you after I rode your face." Corbin told me you raided the house, "Where's my baby Malakai?"

"Somewhere you will never find her."

"Oh, but I will; believe that."

The assailant stands and attempts to escape during the confrontation. Malakai spots him and fires two rounds in his ass and thigh. He shoots another round and watches it bounce a few feet from his head, "Stay put or end up like your partner."

He shifts to Asperilla, "Last chance so stop the madness and leave."

"Fuck you! You want me gone, kill me because I'm not going nowhere."

"I'm tired of fucking with you. I'm coming in; do whatever you have to do."

He steps in and her gun aims at his face.

"Damn, I married the world stupidest man. You are going to die the way you came in this world; naked and afraid."

He doesn't flinch a muscle as she pulls the trigger. The gun jams not once but twice. He walks over, knocks the gun from her hand and pushes her to the floor.

He scans the room for his clothes, "Where is my bag?"

She flips her middle finger and yells," Fuck you!"

He locates it but keeps the weapon drawn on her as he slides on some underwear and shoes.

"Damn, my nuts were cold. Thanks for bringing my guns."

He loads bullets in his 9mm and points at her, "Are you leaving town?"

She twists her fingers through her hair, "You can bury me next to Love Divine and Necole."

"Okay."

He fires two rounds in her chest, and she falls flat on her back. He stoops beside her and closes her eyes.

He returns to the assailant and orders him to give up his cell phone. He scrolls through the contacts and dials Mr. Lancaster, "Corbin, I'm alive and my baby is safe. Asperilla is dead and you are next."

He laughs and responds, "Ayanna mentioned the size of your balls but my position in this city is bigger. I'm tired of playing with you Malakai; bring the bodies and let's end this game. Do I make myself clear?"

"I understand completely but inform Ayanna her body bag is ready. Send the address and I'll show you the size of my balls. They'll be bigger than the ones you almost swallowed."

"Fuck you Mal- "

Malakai terminates the call before he finishes his sentence.

He stares at the assailant and asks, "You wanna live?"

"Yeah, I have a family."

"Me too. Sit tight and don't do anything stupid. My family will tend to you. You have to be camera ready for your interview."

"What interview?"

Malakai punches him in the eye, "Quit asking questions."

He returns to the office, digs his phone out the bag and calls Kryptonite.

"Man, we thought you were dead."

"Almost but I'm good."

"What about Asperilla?"

He looks at her lifeless body, "She's resting; trace my location and send the girls to clean this mess."

"Sounds like the old Malakai is back."

"Yea I guess so and it's a dangerous thing."

"Bout damn time. Do you need me?"

"Nah, stay with Isabella and Grace. I'm not sure what he has planned but I'll contact you. By the way, have them bring some clothes."

"What the hell, you're slinging dick and killing niggas."

"You have no idea the shit I've been through since this morning. Another thing, make sure you find Susan and take her with you."

"Is that all?"

"Yeah, I'll meet ya'll on our favorite island."

"Make them pay and I'll see you there."

Malakai takes a seat, recites poetry and waits for the location.

Chapter 41

Malakai and the disposal team spend most of the morning cleaning up blood and body fragments from the abandoned building. He keeps his promise to the assailant and let him live in exchange for his personal confession. They load Nikki's ashes and Asperilla's body in an unmarked ambulance. He drives the speed limit to the directions of the location.

"You have arrived," the GPS announces.

He honks the horn twice as instructed. A guard comes out the shed, slides the gate open and waves him through the landfill. He drives to the front of the building, parks and retrieve the gifts. He presses the button on the *Stryker Power load* to release the cot on the ground, grabs Nikki's ashes and proceeds to the entrance.

He whistles as he passes the guards with their weapons drawn. The last guard throws his palm in the air. "Stop right there, I need to check your bag."

"Go ahead, nothing but a dead body and ashes."

The guard searches and finds nothing suspicious.

He enters the building and notices Corbin and Ayanna standing in the center of the room. He pauses, looks over his rear shoulder and sees two guards locking the door.

"You sure you want to be locked in with a man with nothing to lose?"

"Do you ever stop bragging? You aren't as tough as you think. On second thought, stay tough because the bidders want to know how well you perform behind bars. Do you have Nikki's remains?" Corbin asks.

"Yeah, what's left of her anyway."

He waves at Ayanna, "Judas how are you doing over there? Finding a tree to hang yourself would be your best option."

She burrows her tongue in Corbin's mouth, wipes his saliva, "Umm, I am protected by the fiercest figure in the city. I will be alright, unlike your dead wife."

Corbin stares at the body bag, "Damn shame what happened to her. I really had plans to drug and toss her in the sex trafficking circus."

He chuckles to himself, "Man, could you imagine the dicks going in and out of her? Those monsters would have eaten her like cannibals. Now back to you Mr. Big Balls, don't you want to know your future?"

"You mean the one about selling me to the highest bidder to benefit your modern-day slave plantation. Nah, I'll pass on that dream."

"The only reason you are alive is because of money. I could have annihilated you months ago but where's the joy in that."

"Corbin, you are a pathetic loser in a business suit. You're a fucking coward planting drugs and criminal charges against black men for money. Ayanna, you can stay hugged up with your boo but ask him what happened to your one-night stand? Did you ever wonder why he never called you again? You were taught to deliver the best pussy and yet, no communication. You think he loves you, I doubt it."

"How does he know about Antonio?" Ayanna asks.

Corbin rubs his hands, winks and wraps his hands around her waist. "Don't worry about his lies; he's trying to tarnish our love."

Malakai reaches inside the bag, pulls out the urn, set it on the floor and rolls it over. "I had her cremated already."

He picks up the urn, twists the lid and inhales her scent, "Ahhh, thank you so much."

He closes and sets it on the table, "Malakai you fulfilled your end of the deal. Your daughter is no longer a factor."

"That's because you don't have her. By the way, how did it feel in jail?"

"This is your last moment of freedom. You should kiss your wife."

"Good idea."

He unzips the bag face level, leans down and kisses her.

"Damn, how long are you going to kiss a corpse?" Corbin asks. "You won a few pieces in our game but I took away your Queen; an eye for an eye. Ayanna take her downstairs to incinerate her body."

"Before I release her, tell her the ugly truth."

"There's no reason to string you along. Ayanna, I have feelings for you, but Nikki is symbolic. You will never replace her existence and as promised, you will receive a piece of the city. Yes, I had Antonio arrested but he's not in jail. I receive a nice payment on the first of each month from his bank account. I'm no different from you and Malakai. I sell innocent black men for profits while you sell pussy."

"I have never sold pussy, I'm a spoken word artist who used to own a club before you kidnapped my daughter and forced me to sign everything over," Malakai proclaims.

Corbin laughs to himself before he boasts more, "You can be whatever you want to be but after today you will become somebody's bitch in a cell block, and I will get paid off your black ass."

"Sounds like some racist shit," Malakai says.

"No, green shit. I love money and if it makes you feel better, I have falsely accused my own kind as well."

Malakai rolls the cot to Ayanna. "Go ahead and burn your old friend while we finish."

"Gladly," Ayanna replies.

"I was expecting for you to die in a blaze of glory. I hired all these guards for nothing."

"What now?" Malakai asks.

I'm glad you asked. "Guards! Prepare the video conference for the bidding and get this money."

The guard forces Malakai against the wall while Corbin sits at a table and begins the bidding. "Good evening gentlemen. As promised, I introduce you to *The Poetic Whore*. Let's the bidding start at $150,000."

Chapter 42

Ayanna is anxious to have Asperilla's body burn to a crisp. She plans on using her ashes as a symbol of authority as the new Queen Pen over the escorts.

Her first mission is to punish Jaz for disrespecting her in the club. Her future dream motivates her to push the cot faster toward the door. She presses the button on the wall to activate the swinging door. "Hurry up and cremate this bitch," she yells rushing into the room.

The technician is prepping the cremation at a slow pace. She places her hands on her hips and yells, "Damn, a turtle moves faster. You were instructed to be ready upon arrival."

He looks over the brim of his glasses and says, "I've been working this job for a long time. Please relax or go to the viewing room."

She throws her hands in the air and responds, "Whatever, just do it."

He continues working until the light flickers before turning pitch black.

"Where are the emergency lights? A dead body and darkness are not my style," she announces.

"Calm down, Ms. Ayanna. We lose power in the basement all the time. It's an old building."

"Fuck you and this building. I'm getting the hell out of here."

She doesn't believe in ghost, but the temperature is decreasing. She shines the light at him and ask, "Are you cold?"

"No, I'm good. Maybe you should go upstairs and see what Mr. Lancaster is doing."

"Great idea."

She shines the phone towards the door and eases down the hall.

"That scare tactic gets them every time," he jokes.

He flips a secret switch on the wall and brightens the room and the outside hallway. He unzips the bag and marvels over her features. "I've never fucked a Hispanic corpse, but I will today."

He bites his lips and squeezes his dick while running his fingers through her hair. He massages her breasts and places a small peck. "Umm, sexy lips," he moans.

He peeps his head out the door to ensure no one is outside. Once satisfied with his privacy, he locks the door, unzips his pants and pulls out his dick.

He strokes a few times to strengthen the erection. He rushes over and unzips the bag to her waist. "Damn, your body is voluptuous."

He reaches his hand under her shirt, fondles her nipples, and masturbates. "Yeah, getting this dick ready for your sexy dead ass."

He leans in for another kiss. "Let me taste your lips one more time."

He inches closer and blows his breath over her face. "Say you want me," he chants.

Her eyes pop open and she jabs the stainless-steel dagger in his temple. "Yeah Papi. I want you… dead."

She kisses his cheeks, twists the knife deeper, yanks it out and watches him slump to the floor clutching the side of his head.

She unzips the bag and hops down in front of him. "Ewww, you are nasty as hell; down here fucking dead bodies and shit."

She plunges the knife into his Adam's apple. "Swallow my blade... sick bastard."

She stands and unzips an undetected compartment in the body bag. She retrieves her gun, attaches her earpiece, and places a gas mask in her backpack.

The earpiece is synced to the team outside the building. "Mei, come in," she announces.

"Damn, Malakai's plan of faking your death was brilliant. We have Corbin's confession recorded and downloaded," Mei confirms.

"Ok, I'm getting Malakai; create a diversion for me, and let's get this shit over with it."

"We gotcha, the first beep is your warning and the second one is the fireworks outside," Mei responds.

"Roger that!"

Asperilla rushes out the room but pauses at the door. She returns to the technician and snatches the knife out of his throat.

"Puta!" She yells and spits in his face.

She wipes the blood on his shirt, tucks the knife and sneaks up the stairwell. She makes it to the top and peeps out the window. The guards are relaxing and not paying attention. She chuckles and thinks *lazy ass security.*

She takes a deep inhale, chambers her first round and eases to the door. Her radio beeps once to take cover and put on her gas mask. She ducks behind a table and waits.

The second beep comes and seconds later the ambulance explodes creating confusion between the guards.

She tosses the tear gas in the hallway so the smoke can fill the door entrance. She waits a few minutes before rushing and kicking it open. She squeezes the trigger and the bullet hits the first guard in the head and he slumps to the floor. She steps over him and strikes the other guard in the chest and between the eyes.

She keeps her aim on Corbin and Ayanna as she makes her way to Malakai. She gives him the gun, removes her mask and shakes her hair loose. "Buenas Noches muthafuckers," she greets.

"You sup... Suppose to be dead," Ayanna stutters.

"I was but the devil sent me back to torment your ass." She points at Corbin. "Checkmate!"

"I'm a District attorney and they will give you the death penalty for killing me," he speaks flamboyantly adjusting his tie.

Malakai lowers the gun. "You are right."

Corbin laughs before responding, "I'm always right."

He shoots Corbin in the knee. He falls and wraps his hand around his kneecap, "Aww, shit, you will pay for this."

Ayanna falls to her knees, interlocking her fingers and begs, "I'm sorry."

Asperilla walks over and punches her in the face, "Bitch please, save the fake dramatic shit. No one is shooting your ass."

Malakai walks to the computer and collects all the data from the bidders running the corrupted prison systems.

"You think you can get away with this shit, I'll put a bigger price tag on your head. You better kill me now because I'm coming for you."

Malakai looks down at him and laughs before shooting him in the other kneecap. "You are going to jail and every case you represented will be expunged. You are out of moves Mr. Lancaster."

Malakai counts his fingers. "I have your bidder's info, your confessions, witnesses, and your Assistance DA. You and I both know this location is off the radar. The police aren't coming to save your ass this time."

"Okay, let's make a deal. I'll let bygones be bygones."

Malakai looks at Ayanna and shakes his head in disgust, "Nah, I tried to forgive once and betrayed; never again."

Chapter 43

Malakai sits in the back of the transport van with his head dropped between his legs. He hasn't spoken a word since they departed the landfill.

Asperilla rubs his shoulder and coos, "Baby, it's almost over."

He weeps, "Yeah, I'm tired of living this life."

He lifts his head, stares in her eyes and speaks a soft tone, "Asperilla, my life as a *Poetic Whore* was fucking women and spontaneous adventures. Why did you stay?"

"Because I was fucking the same bitches," she responds.

She kisses his cheek and admits, "I love you Malakai and you are my soulmate."

"You never thought about killing me?"

She didn't respond.

"What the fuck! Are you serious right now?"

"Calm down, I'm only joking."

She whispers in his ear, "We need to hurry. My pussy is soaking from all this mission impossible shit."

"Oh, you are getting some dick soon…real soon."

"Yes," she shouts like a kid in a candy store.

Her face turns sour when her eyes connect to Ayanna. She stares her down and spreads her legs. "I should make you taste your creator one last time. You are the dumbest hoe I have ever seen. Mei, are we almost there?"

"Five minutes," she responds.

"Great! Because I'm sick of looking at this bitch." Asperilla sits back and mumbles, "I can't wait to bury your ass."

Malakai lifts his head, smiles, and rubs her thigh. "Patience baby. She deserves something unique for her final stay."

He massages deeper and she grabs his hands to rub her throbbing pussy.

"What the hell you are doing?" He asks.

"Trying to get finger fucked before the van stops."

"You are wild as hell Asperilla."

"I forgot to mention, Corbin's technician loves to fuck women corpses."

"Get out of here."

"I'm not lying. He was feeling all over me and shit with his nasty ass."

He burst out laughing, "You and your damn adventures. Sounds like a story you can tell Jaz and Cherry."

She shrugs her shoulders and responds, "Maybe."

The van slows down to make a turn and coasts along the road. It comes to a complete halt and Mei yells, "We're here."

Meiying opens the passenger door and runs to the rear to unlock it.

Asperilla stands from her seat, unties Ayanna's hands and assists her to the edge of the van. She lifts her leg and kicks Ayanna in the butt. "Get your ass out."

She falls to the payment and rolls over. Asperilla steps down and unfastens her gag ball.

"You don't have to do this. I know you have love for me. I'll leave town… go to another country, whatever you want, I promise to do it," Ayanna pleads.

"Bring Corbin out here," Asperilla orders.

Malakai loosens the strap and escorts him, "Come on Mr. Lancaster, let me show you what happens when you fuck with me."

Malakai unties his gag, "You have permission to speak."

"I underestimated you. I watched you set your house on fire, stabbed Malakai and destroyed Love Divine gravesite," Corbin admits to Asperilla.

"I would have put a bullet in Malakai's head for my daughter. By the way, the tombstone was fake. Malakai orchestrated everything to gain your trust. His own team didn't know half of the shit he was planning. He wanted to make it feel real as his favorite movie, *Last Knights*," she explains. "Your arrogance was your biggest downfall."

"Enough chatting get this divorce party started," Malakai yells.

Mei and Meiying keep their weapons drawn on Corbin & Ayanna as they walk in front of them.

Ayanna pauses once she sees the first car she purchased as an escort and her recent vehicle. She turns her head over her shoulder. "What are my cars doing here?"

"To celebrate the ride of your life."

"What does that mean?"

Asperilla sucker punches her and yells, "Bitch, shut up. Malakai, enough of this poetic shit. Ayanna, your Judas ass will experience a gruesome death."

Asperilla pushes between the cars. "Get down."

She hesitates and attempts to beg for mercy one last time, "Please don't do this. I don't want to die."

"You wanted to feed my firstborn to an anaconda, and you think I'm supposed to forgive you; Go to hell!"

"Ya'll bitches think you can eat my pussy and stab me in the back. You can join Pandora's headless ass."

She drags Ayanna by her arms to the first vehicle and wraps the chains around her wrist. She grabs her legs and adjust the chains from the second car to her ankles. She secures it to their hitching posts, squats, and kisses Ayanna.

She releases, opens the car door and starts the ignition. She slams her foot on the gas and the engine roars causes her to panic and screams, "No, Asperilla…don't do this."

She shifts the car in drive and lightly press the accelerator, pulling the chain around her ankles tighter. The car coasts a few inches stretching her body.

She rolls down the window and yells, "Ayanna, you did this to yourself."

She thinks about the fun they had back in the day. She laughs before mumbling, "Divorce means you get half of everything you put in."

She stomps the gas pedal to the floor; the chain stretches and rips Ayanna's waist from her torso. She turns off the ignition, steps out and walks behind the car. Her legs were attached to the hitch, leaving a trail of blood and guts back to the other car. She died with her eyes and mouth open.

Asperilla leans near her ear and whispers, "You picked the wrong team."

She skips and dances. "Ya'll saw that shit. Corbin, you should have left us alone after Nikki died. Mei and Meiying, keep an eye on him while we dispose of this. If he moves…catheterize his dick with a barrel rod."

Chapter 44

He does a final sweep around the area to confirm Ayanna's murder wouldn't come back to haunt him.

He's anxious to return to the city and meet the authorities with Corbin.

"Alright, everything looks good; let's go."

His pulls out the phone, looks at the number, and presses the talk button. "We are on our way with the package."

"Are you sure prison is the best thing for this grimy manipulating muthafucker?" Asperilla asks.

"No, he deserves death, but he'll pay for stealing innocent lives."

Malakai closes his eyes and silently recite a poem until they reach the city. He finishes his third stanza and doesn't remember anything after the last cadence.

Asperilla wakes him by punching him in the shoulder. "We are here. Get your ass up!" she shouts.

He yawns, wipes his face and responds, "This has been the longest 48 hours of my life."

He retrieves the blindfold and ties it around Corbin's eyes.

"Malakai, it's not too late to take the deal. We could run this city together; think about the money we can make," Corbin brides.

"Sounds good but you are forgetting one thing."

"What's that?"

"I hate this city. It has too many bad memories for me. You can keep your deal and save it for your new cellmate."

"You are making a big mistake."

He ignores the offer and ushers him to the awaiting officers. He gives him one hard shove and Corbin trips over his feet and falls. "Get this piece of shit out of my sight."

Malakai walks back to the van and hears him screaming at the top of his lungs. "It's not over Malakai. You should have killed me."

He climbs in the back of the van and ditch it at the nearest chop shop.

Mei kisses Malakai on the cheek. "I'm glad Graciana is safe and we are alive."

Meiying kisses Asperilla and refuses to break it until Malakai steps in. "Hey, that's enough; quit trying to steal my wife."

Meiying rubs her hands between her thighs. "Only reminding her what the Far East can offer."

"Whatever, with your lying ass."

Asperilla hugs Mei & Meiying. "Thank you for helping us. If we met a couple of years earlier, I would have three tongues in me right now."

Malakai glances at the sky and knows in a few hours the sun will shine. "Listen, we could chat until morning, but I need some alone time with my wife."

"That's cool, we have an early flight anyway. Thanks for booking us a private plane because *TSA* wouldn't understand a bag full of dicks."

"You are welcome," Malakai answers.

They exchange hugs and depart in different vehicles.

Malakai has reservation at the casino and ready to unwind. He chats with Asperilla until they reach the valet and exits the car. He grabs the keys at the counter and ride the elevator to their suite.

Upon entering the room, she strips and prepares the shower. "You can join me if you like," she hollers.

Malakai quickly accepts the invitation. He turns on some music and steps in. They take turns washing, sharing kisses, and massaging each other sensitive spots.

Asperilla points at the hot tub. "Do you want to make love right here?"

He reminisces about his dream of Asperilla drowning him while eating her. He shakes his head from side to side. "Nah, the bed is good."

He scoops her into his arms and carries her to the love place. He climbs on top, stares into her eyes and whispers, "I love you."

"No, Papi, you love eating this pussy," she replies pushing his head between her thighs.

He plants his face and tugs on her clitoris, pulling with his teeth and returning with a slurp.

She massages the top of his head, lifts her right leg in the air and uses her shins against his neck to push him deeper. He pounds his face in her pussy and listens to the gushy sounds of her wetness. He spreads her lips wider and inserts his index finger.

"Eat your chocho," she moans.

She grips his ears as she bucks. He inserts another one, sucking greedily and finger fucking her faster.

"Oh shit! I don't wanna cum soon."

She slaps his head, attempting to make him stop but he's in an oral zone.

He gyrates his fingers deeper, causing her back to arch as he feasts harder.

"Aww fuck," she yells.

"Mal...Mal...Malakai."

She squirts and juices splash in his nose. He catches and holds some in his mouth. He waits until her flush is complete and swallows her love.

They tongue wrestle for a minute until he retracts the kiss. "I was prepared to make love tonight until you push my head down."

"Save the love making shit for another time. Find me a song to fuck to."

He flips the radio, jumps on the bed and pops his dick in her face. She kisses the tip, deep throat it down and back. She spits on his head and opens her pussy. "Put it in now," she groans and winds her hips.

"I'm not being gentle," he warns.

He flips her over, enters from behind, and rocks back and forth. He presses his hand on the top of her ass and pounds deeper and harder. She reaches behind and spreads her ass cheeks apart giving full access to murder her pussy. He takes full advantage of the opening and fucks her faster.

"Oh my God," she yells.

He refuses to stop. Her knees give out and she falls on the bed. He grabs her throat and rams her pussy.

"I wanna ride," she screams.

He thrusts more before sliding out and rolling on his back.

She inserts and rides his dick. Her titties flop near his face and he snatches and slurps it. Her ass smacks against his thighs. She inserts a finger into her pussy, pulls it out, and makes him suck it. Her hips rise, and her pussy comes to the tip of his head before slamming down.

"Aww fuck baby, ride this dick," he yells.

He wraps his arms around her waist, pulls her down and thrusts this dick. She grinds in circles as he brushes the hair away from her face.

"Oh, you are fucking now. Fuck this pussy Malakai. Yes…Yes…Yes…"

He breathes harder as he digs in her walls.

She slows down, flops over and throws her legs in the air.

He inserts his dick from the side and penetrates faster as she massages her clit. He pinches her nipples as his dick slides in and out.

She looks over her shoulder and watches the determination on his face. "Yes, get that nut baby. Get that nut for Mami."

He slows his thrusts and gives it nice and steady. He takes his time to enjoy the love strokes.

She turns her head and kisses him in the mouth.

He slides out, bends her legs backward and speeds up again.

"No mercy bitch take this dick," he grunts.

"I'm taking it, Papi."

"Take it all."

Drool leaks from his mouth as he thrust into the air.

"Oh fuck, don't stop."

He listens to her commands and snatches a fist full of her hair and pounds forcibly.

She cums and he waits for her body to descend before beating his dick. She plays in her pussy from watching his dick into the palm of his hand until he feels the nut cumming.

He takes her by surprise by entering again and thrusting a few more times before releasing one of the hardest nuts inside of her.

He shakes and yells, "Aww shit, I love your pussy."

He flops on his back.

She lies her head on his chest while he massages her ass cheeks and plays with her hair until they fall asleep.

Chapter 45

Malakai sits outside a café in Venice writing a poem until the ladies meet him. He takes a break, stares at the scene and reflects on the 2 years since leaving Tampa.

He gave up pussy and destructions for an exotic and beautiful scenery. He raises his daughter in peace and is a replica of Asperilla's sassiness speaking Spanish and English.

Isabella refused to go home so he made sure she enrolled in college to earn her degree online as she travels with them.

Kryptonite, Mei, & Meiying went back to their illegal activities and still trying to entice him to rejuvenate their business.

His agreement worked out with Ms. Drummond. She is the new District Attorney and Kryptonite's fuck buddy whenever he's in town.

His phone vibrates on the table. "Humph, speaking of Ms. Drummond," he mumbles.

"Good Morning Susan, how can I help you?"

"I know you're off the grid for a while, but it seems our friend is ready for another game of revenge. He sent a letter to my office this morning."

"It seems living was a mistake. No worries, I'll handle it."

He put the phone down and types another verse on his poem. He stops writing and admires the view one last time before texting Asperilla. *"Call me before you leave the hotel, I'm going for a walk."*

"Ok."

He saves his work, packs his laptop, and leaves. He slides his shades on to block the sun rays and strolls through an alleyway.

Even though he has been off the grid, he keeps close ties with Corbin's release. They claimed not enough evidence to sustain the case and only gave him 2 years in a secured facility for becoming an informant. He spilled his guts on all the bidders and crooked city officials. His punk ass went to a fucking resort and now he's out on probation starting shit.

He walks a mile down the road and does a secret knock on the warehouse door. A bearded brute man opens reminding him of *Braun Strowman* from *WWE*.

"She's expecting you," he says and steps aside for him to pass.

Malakai walks down the hall and up the stairs to her office. She stands from her desk wearing a sleeveless halter, lace mini skirt falling to her shins, and complimented strappy heels.

She swings her jet-black hair to the side, walks over, and kisses him on both cheeks. "Benvenuto Malakai," she greets.

"Good Morning Francesca, it has been a long time."

"Time hasn't erased your sexiness. It's been almost 10 years. I was shocked when you told me about your visit."

"Yeah, I've been traveling, and this is one of my stops."

"How's the family?"

"Everyone is lovely, I can't complain."

"How can I help you?"

"I need remote access from your computer to conduct a video conference."

"Sure, it's in the green room. I can escort you."

He kisses her cheeks, "Thank you so much."

He follows her to another office with a sign for authorized personnel.

She opens the door and slaps him on the ass, "Umm, firm like I remember."

He smiles and points outside the door, "Francesca, get out."

"Okay, I'll be down the hall if you need me."

They used to fuck but stopped when she moved to Venice. He helped establish her operations and secret business partners.

He shifts his thoughts, closes the door and sets up the communication. He hired a friend with an IT background to work the same day he sent Ayanna.

He sent Corbin's access codes for his network. Malakai hacked through the connection and wait for the conference. It connects successfully and he appears on the main conference screen interrupting their secret briefing.

"Good morning Mr. Lancaster," Malakai addresses.

"How the hell you infiltrated my system? I'm glad you are ready to play but this time I'm taking you out for good."

"I noticed you hired a few mercenaries. I guess your last security team wasn't up to par."

"Fuck you," Corbin yells slamming his fist on the table.

"No need to get upset. I know you are trying to trace this call, but it won't work plus I won't be long. Do you recall I mentioned bringing your bitch back?"

"What the hell are you talking about?" Corbin asks.

"I never cremated Nikki. She's buried under your conference table and have been waiting for you to get out of jail."

Corbin jumps from his seat and screams, "Help me move this table."

He watches them slide the table, rip the loose wood panels and sees a black body bag.

Corbin unzips and discovers the remains. He pulls out a note that reads, "*It's easy to forgive but letting a person to live is forbidden.*"

Malakai gives him a moment to reminisce. He grabs the burner phone and punches in the numbers to trigger the bomb. He pauses for a moment of silence before killing off his nemesis.

"Times up," he whispers before pressing send. The hidden phone in Nikki's body bag triggers the bomb and the video screen goes dark.

Malakai waits a few minutes before checking his FB feed. He scrolls to Jaz's timeline for the incineration of Corbin's office suite. He watches the devastation as the news team and emergency responders arrive. He logs off, packs up the equipment and leaves.

He erases Corbin's death from his mind and focuses on his date with three beautiful ladies.

"Are you still getting dressed?"

"Malakai, you're on speakerphone so don't say anything crazy."

He hears his daughter in the background yelling, "Papi...Papi."

"I have developed deep patience over the years. When you all are finished, let's sightseeing.

"I'm sure they would enjoy it."

"What about you?"

"I would prefer fucking and serenade music in a gondola through the city."

His dick jumps in his from her thoughts. "Baby, you have my attention. We can make that happen. Alright, I'm heading back to the cafe. I'll meet you there. I love you Asperilla."

"I love you too Malakai."

Graciana screams in the background, "I love you Papi."

"Love you too Graciana."

He ends the call, returns to the café and finds a seat. He opens his computer and focuses on his unfinished poem. Sometimes he wonders if he should write a novel about a poet running an escort service with his sexy diabolical wife.

He chuckles and thinks, *"Nah, I'm sure no one would read that shit; I'll stick to poetry."*

Flenardo Speaks

Flenardo is the Author of The Poetic Whore & Married to the Pen. He's an ordinary man who foreplays his dreams into reality with creative strokes of imaginative superpowers.

Thank you for reading Forbidden Forgiveness. You are welcome to post amazon reviews and share your social media love with friends.

I love chatting with all my supporters. You can connect with me by joining my newsletter for upcoming novels, tours, & book signings at http://freknardo.com/

ACKNOWLEDGEMENTS

Praises and blessings to the creator for giving me the gift of poetry and writing.

Creolistic Ink & Ms. Adrina Smith, thanks for burning the midnight oil with me over the years and encouraging me to be a team player.

Alesia Barcus, thanks for reading Married to the Pen and coming up with Forbidden Forgiveness.

Tonyela Masterpiece Arphul, thanks for accepting my invitation to become the feature model for the book cover. I love reading your work and cheering for your success as well. https://www.masterpiecepoetry.com/about

Soul Wire Cafe, (Jackson, Ms) thanks for allowing me to perform poetry in your city.

Monique Christians, thanks for treating me as a superstar. I will never forget the day you asked me to sign my autograph on a napkin. Thanks for introducing me to Tootie Harmon, a loyal supporter, and friend.

Sherrbear Stewart, Takeshia Smith, & Stephanie Brooks. Thanks for taking road trips to watch me perform in Atlanta and Anniston.

Tasha Reed, thanks for giving me the opportunity to perform at your wedding and telling your friends about my novels.

Suzen Robertson, thanks for allowing me to be a part of the Catalyst and the Art scene in Anniston.

Richard White, thanks for bringing your work to the poetry shows and becoming one of the coolest friends on the planet.

Kristy Hill Farmer & The Peerless Saloon staff, thanks for the love over six years.

Laydee Shebeau, you are the best supporter in the world. I can't wait to purchase your book.

Tameka Smith, (ARIA) thanks for being the best and always sharing your stories.

Eric Hall, thanks for leaving the big city to support me.

Special thanks to Charmaine for allowing me to write and spread love with the world. I love you baby!

Candice Theresa, Candice Jackson, Carolyn Jordan, Olympia George (busting out your window), Shemika Davis, Author MJL, Jessica Driskell, Church Da Poet, Ebonique AKA Lady Picasso,
Betty Battles, Antoinette LaToya, Narada Culpepper, Fantashia Smith, Gloria Prince, LTC Sumlin, Rita Chandelar, Melvin Richards, MyReality, Natosha Gray, Sygrid Beard, Tanilya Dawson, Tunisia Necole, Vanesha Crawford, KC & Holly Oswalt, Ken Guthrie, A Maint Shelly, & LaTasha Jackson

You can never capture the love of everyone but when you purchase your copy. I promise to write an autograph worthy of an Oscar. Thanks for the love, encouragements, and support.

www.ingramcontent.com/pod-product-compliance
Lightning Source LLC
Chambersburg PA
CBHW022200170626
46807CB00005B/2280